HOW TO STOP LOVING SOMEONE

Also by the author

History Lessons
The World Before Mirrors
Here on Old Route 7
We Who Live Apart

STORIES

Joan Connor

HOW TO STOP LOVING SOMEONE

A LeapLit Book
Leapfrog Literature
Leapfrog Press
Teaticket, Massachusetts

A LeapLit Book
Leapfrog Literature

Published in 2011 in the United States by
Leapfrog Press LLC
PO Box 2110
Teaticket, MA 02536
www.leapfrogpress.com

Distributed in the United States by
Consortium Book Sales and Distribution
St. Paul, Minnesota 55114
www.cbsd.com

First Edition

Library of Congress Cataloging-in-Publication Data

Connor, Joan, 1954-
How to stop loving someone / by Joan Connor. -- 1st ed.
p. cm.
Short stories.
ISBN 978-1-935248-20-0 (alk. paper)
I. Title.
PS3553.O514255H69 2011
813'.54--dc22
2011027710

Printed in the United States of America

To my family and all the others whom I love.
You know who you are.

Contents

HOW TO STOP LOVING SOMEONE

Men in Brown

THIS IS HOW BAD IT'S GOTTEN: I dream about the U.P.S. man. I order household items I neither need nor want: extendible fan blade dusters (I do not have a fan); silver serving spoons (I do not have dinner parties); tulip bulbs (weeds strangle my flower beds); and this morning, complicated underwear with clips and flying buttresses and lace and thongs and garters. (I already own thirty-two Miracle bras, and on me they look like penance). And, yes, I regret it already. When the discreet brown-papered package arrives will *he* snicker at me, his brown eyes, eyes the flavor of bitter brickle chocolate, lick over me, knowing, secretive, brown, his black shock of hair sending shock waves down my spine? Oh, heart be still. Men in uniform. What *was* I thinking?

It began innocently enough. I joined a book club; I just wanted to belong, to belong to a club. Club, it sounds so chummy, so hail-fellow-well-met. Except that I hate crowds, so I joined a book club. I could be a member but stay home. I am something of an agoraphobe, but I am a claustrophobe, too. I rattle around in my house like a stray thought. I spend unhealthy lengths of time staring out my windows. An agoraphobic-claustrophe, you can imagine why this might be a problem. But once a month, the books arrived, and once a month I could leaf through the catalogues, the cookbooks and self-help books and fill in the tidy little order form with my fastidious fine-tipped pen. The books were a comfort. And once a month the brown truck, the neat little brown truck bumped up my dirt road like a parcel with wheels. The little brown truck with its matching driver, nicely groomed and bearing gifts.

I looked forward to the monthly delivery, anticipated it, counted on it like the full moon, as predictable and regular as the electric bill. Then I got zapped.

I was staring out the window, as was my wont, expecting my latest club order, *A Brief History of Dish Washing Gloves*, when the familiar truck thumped up my drive. But wait. What was this? This was not my militarily neat driver. Who was this man in brown with the Love-Me-Tender lock which he whipped back as he flung open the rear door? His lean brown legs scissored up my walk, cutting my breath short. The knock.

I opened the door. "Gack," I said like a cartoon cat with its tail in a wood chipper. My mouth clogged with wet sawdust.

I slipped into his eyes like a strawberry dipped in fondue chocolate. Delicious mud-pie eyes. Drowning in cocoa syrup. "Do I have to sign?" I asked, but my oral-motor muscles were shot. "Goo," I drooled. "Grobble?" I wiped my chin.

He chuckled. He knew. I am sure that he knew. They always know. He bounced the book in his palms. "Your package."

"Ung," I thanked him.

He tucked his pad under his arm. His hands were brown, too, and strong. I imagined him on his Saturdays off, doing brown things, his hands in loam or in his yard creosoting timbers, his shirt off, his chest turning chestnut under the spanning chestnut tree. I swooned. I braced myself against the doorjamb.

"I belong, too," he said. He nodded at the package.

Heavenly days. He read. All that well-packaged pulchritude, and he could read, too.

"Pynchon's latest was more accessible than the previous one. What's the title?" He jutted his star-studded chin at my package.

"Huh?"

"The title?"

I sank to my enfeebled chin in the mushy brown slurp of his eyes.

"What are you planning on reading there?"

I stared at the package in my hand with lickerish aphasia. Lust lapse. I snapped my synapses back together. "Immanuel Kant," I said. "The complete works."

We both stared at the tiny package. The Categorical Diminutive.

"The miracle of digitization," I said. "E-books."

He chuckled again, made a cute little salute with that Saturday tanned hand and said, "Be seeing you," and sauntered off in his bister serge, my heart a lurch behind him.

That was how it began. I tried to reason with myself. He was just a dun-colored suit on a new route. But I began ordering more books, more dusters, more pie servers, more satin tap pants. What was I doing? I imagined myself tap-dancing my heart out on little Jack Horner's plummy pie while reciting sonnets, the couplets rhyming like door chimes, like thee and me. I inked in order forms, one a day, then two, before I knew it, seven or eight a day, and, driving to the post office I startled, did triple and quadruple takes, thinking that I spotted his sporty van jaunting along the road, here, no there, turning the corner in the corner of my eye.

It had been a while since I'd been interested in anyone. When I first stopped teaching and moved to my home here in the Vermont hills, I thought, that's it. I had a free lance job editing text books. No more dates.

That was before the root canal. While I gagged on drains and drills and torture devices, my dentist told me about his divorce. He asked me out to dinner. He had trays full of sharp instruments at his disposal. I had a mouth full of hardware. How could I say no?

As I recall, the date ended miserably on the edge of a snowy field in his parked truck. When he tried to kiss me, all I could think about was dental hygiene. Had I flossed that morning? He told me that one of his fillings picked up a local radio station. He had a metal plate in his head, a consequence of brain surgery. He kept humming. *The Copacabana*, I think. I kept praying for the tooth fairy to swoop down, whisk me home, and tuck me under my own pillow. There was no second date.

About a month later driving back from a power-struggle lunch with my publisher, I stopped at The Pioneer House for a double. A man at the end of the bar sent up another. A double double. He sidled onto the neighboring stool. A Vet, it turned out, Viet Nam. Also with a plate in his head. Strafed by a detonated mine, he claimed. Two men with steel plates in their heads. What a coinky-dink, I thought, as I drove myself home on a four-laned highway that had been two-laned four hours ago. Double vision.

But the third one. It gave me pause. High school history teacher whose chapter on *The Age of the Iron Horse* I was editing, he proposed marriage promptly, over his third martini. Had a huge settlement from a car accident, ready to settle down. Head injury, yep, steel plate in his head.

Once, you think—how sad. Twice, you think—odd. Thrice, you think—hey, wait a minute. Is there a lot of this going on out there? Occurrence, repetition, pattern.

He said that he was thinking of retitling the chapter, *The Iron Age*. I said, "Bad move," and made mine. I was out the door and on the road faster than you can say, "Desperado."

And I was desperate, desperate to be gone, to be golden, to be history. Steel Plate Man? The superhero of litigious geek myth? I'd never be that desperate.

Then there was Walter. We met at a Parents Without Partners mixer. We were both just trying to pass. Childless, we found out after we skipped out on the line dancing, both of us. One two skip to my Lou. We drank Manhattans in Rutland at the Holiday Inn, Cosmopolitans in Cowtown. "Children," Walter said, "are the black hole of conversation."

"Children," I said, "are the black hole of life."

We started seeing each other, and it worked out pretty well because we didn't like each other very much. No fretting by the phone, waiting for the other to call. No bitten fingernails. Vinous recriminations, whine and roses. We caught the occasional movie, tangled each other's sheets, went Dutch on Scotch. It went along fine until he dumped me.

"I can't see you any more."

"Can you see me any less?"

"I'm serious."

"About whom?"

"I've met someone."

"Where?"

"She's a model. A model and a psychiatrist."

This was unlikely. "Where did you say you met?"

"I didn't."

"You didn't meet."

"I didn't say."

This went on for a while. Walter was serious; he was also seriously insane. He had met this therapo-babe in a chat room. A lingerie model, she claimed. A shrink, she said. Shrink-wrapped maybe—Walter sent me a Neiman Marcus catalogue with a wispy waspy blonde model on the cover in a corduroy Christmas jumper with a snowman embroidered on the bib. No self-respecting woman wears a corduroy Frostie, even for a photo-shoot, even if she teaches second grade. I tried to imagine her Santa-panties, her figgy pudding.

"That's her," Walter said when he called next.

"How do you know?"

"She told me."

"Walter." I tried. It wasn't jealousy. As I said, it had only worked out because we didn't like each other much. I explained that she could be anybody, a man. A telepathological liar. That it was unlikely that she was Victoria's unkept secret and an expert on and off the couch. That was male fantasy, email fantasy. Chat room chatter. Electronic locker room banter.

But Walter was serious. He was trying to figure out if he could support her and her three kids.

"Walter, if she 's a model and. . . ."

But he would hear none of it. He was looking at houses with four bedrooms, bungalows, shotguns. He was looking at flights to New Orleans.

Next call: "She's back-pedaling."

Sur-prahze. Sur-prahze, Gomer.

"She's not sure that she wants to meet."

Uh-huh.

Next call: "Everything she told me wasn't true."

Well, gadzooks.

"But some of it was true. I know that there's something there. We've been talking on the phone every day."

"Never at night?"

"She has kids."

"YOU'VE *never* talked to her at night."

"I'm going down there. If she's even one-third as good as I think, I've got to know."

Walter flew down, followed his heart to New Orleans and came home with a steel plate in it. He'd holed up for three days in a cheap hotel near her husband's office. She was not a lingerie model, looked nothing like the corduroy cutie on the catalogue. She had modeled hats once in junior high for a local department store's Spring Fling. She was not a psych-therapist although she had taken a counseling course in Junior College before she got married, and she was likely certifiable. Now she was married and wanted out, and was husband-hunting for number one's replacement, casting her inter-net on the wide electronic sea. But she and Walter? Two blips who passed in the night. She was not one-third as good, one quarter, one-twentieth, one-one-thousandth, one googolplexth as good as he thought.

Walter was disappointed, but he recovered quickly. He asked me out the following Saturday. But I declined. I didn't dislike him enough any longer. What could I tell him? That I didn't know that he had that much hope, that much capacity for delusion in him? I could love a man like that, so I never returned his call. He married the Holiday Inn hostess two months later.

But the psycho-model haunted me. In the hypnagogic dusk, the oneiric purple evenings of late fall, she glimmered over the silage, like summer's last firefly, a fleeting thought. I could understand an e-flirtation, an e-seduction, an e-mendacity. But to move from e to actuality, that was beyond my comprehension. How could she show up at some quickie motel, wearing her face, her flesh, all the while knowing that Walter, her e-paramour, trembled behind door number two (the brass number slightly askew) expecting an entirely other e-babe to enter his embrace, expecting to grab the brass ring and exchange it for a diamond one. Surely she knew, one knock and she'd blown her glossy cover. Did she think that he'd overlook the catalogue ink and love her on the instant for herself? Was that optimism or crass brass?

Bang the conundrum loudly. Herald in the new me. That was that. I was done with dating. Really done this time. Overdone, tough with gristle, charred to the bone.

How to Stop Loving Someone

Hard as hardtack. Down to brass tacks: no more dates.

But that was before, before Mr. U.P.S. rolled into my driveway, my life, my heart. And it was just time now, a week or two, before those orders started rolling in, rolling rolling rolling, keep those brown trucks rolling, rolling down my dateless driveway. And they did. They do.

So how to explain why I hide in my own closet or crouch behind my couch whenever I hear a car bump up the driveway or catch a glimpse of the brown truck nosing to a stop in front of my garage, leaving my Mister U.P.S. to leave a parcel tucked into a forlorn door, unsigned for, unwelcomed, unloved. How to explain that, after the plume of dust settles in the driveway, that then, that only then, I scurry out of the closet or scuttle from behind the couch to retrieve my parcel with its plastic daisy sink stopper within only to press the corrugated cardboard against my chest, trying to recover the warmth of his palms, his brown hands against brown paper. I live in sepia tint like a curling photograph.

When I should be editing, I find myself staring out windows again, willing the little brown truck up my driveway so that I can dash into my closet before he reaches my door. Oh mysterious workings of the human heart.

I named him UPS, Mr. Ups. Up. Heart rate up. Pulse up. Attitude up and up and soaring. Up, the launching pad to my heart. Up my hopes and raised my eyes. My brown clad lad, my star ascendant. My pretty package, Mr. Ups.

When you live alone, you can keep your own schedule. This morning I've been editing the Iron Horse chapter, steel plate number three, since five a.m.. At ten I decide to color my gray and wash my sins away. Halfway through my shower, the tap head starts spitting pellets. Power must have gone out. I lurch out of the stall. My feet freeze to the floor. I can't find my towel and have a head full of dye. I grab the nearest thing I can find to plunk onto my head while I scramble, naked, chattering in quest of towel. I twist my mop into a padded mailer and dash for the linen closet. Sweet Jesus, it is cold. I emanate steam. Dry ice. Then I hear it—a distant rumble in crescendo, crescendo. Quick. What? Hide.

I up-end a wingchair in the living room, and, trying to compress my body into the size of an ice cube, I weld myself to the chairback. At least I forget that I am cold, but my heart stabs me like a jousting icicle. Calm down, I reason with myself.

But I can hear in the purr in the drive, the brown cozy cat of the purr that it is my package man, the van, the vanguard of my fantasies. Hush, I say to my roving mercenary marauder of a heart.

I hear the knock. My heart rocks. The knock again. I cling to my chairback with the fervor of a capsized sailor.

"Kristina," he calls.

How does he know my name? Of course, the packages. But I stay mute although my pounding heart is eloquent.

Knock and knock. "Kristina? Kristina, I saw your car in the drive."

My ice-cube body is melting into the upholstery. Faster, I urge, trying to become smaller, trying to shrink. Alice had it easy; she could just toss back a drink.

"Kristina, is everything okay?"

Okay? Okay? Why doesn't he go away and take that black licorice whip of hair with him? But I am a sucker for sweets. An all-day sucker, a sucker for succor. "Fine," I say. "Everything's fine." My voice sounds as thin as a spaghetti strap slipping from a shoulder.

"I have a package for you."

My skin is grafting to the toile, weaving itself into the figured willows. "Swell," I call.

"Do you want me to set it inside the door?"

"No," I call. I try to sound breezy, cute, the way that I imagine cotillion blondes sound on holiday at sea resorts, but it is difficult to sound breezy when one is freezing to a chairback like a tongue to a January mailbox. "Just set it on the stoop."

"Could I come in? I wanted to ask you something. Something else?"

"What?" I aim for breezy again. "Ask away."

"Um, I'd really like to ask this in person."

"I'm busy. Indisposed. Book deadline, you know." All this yelling with my stomach pressed into a pellet leaves me panting. "Awful these publishers. Pressure cookers, they are. Task masters. Regular slave drivers."

And then the knock. Only directly behind me. Back door. Not front. Next to the sidelights, lovely for light, those slot windows—with muntins.

This is one of those moments in life, rare. A moment which demands composure. A moment which reveals to one one's iron resources, one's grace. My grace is buck naked and pointed at the muntined window, wet and shivering, married to an upset chair, with a padded brown mailer on its head and snakes of brown dye

Medusa-tressing down its cheeks as it hollers into tufted toile. My iron resources, likewise.

In such a moment one ponders decorum. One ponders decorum because decorum is decidedly what one lacks. One hopes that the padded envelope on one's head will look deliberate, maybe even rakish, a fashion innovation as one peels one's self from the dye-stained toile and stands tall, tall and naked, chicken-fleshed, plucked by cold, and adopts a devil-may-care stance which one recalls from a model on a Neiman Marcus catalogue and carefully, sans souci, calls, "Coming," which the caller can plainly witness himself through the panel windows.

U.P.S. must send their trainees to a boot camp in Iraq; he doesn't blink.

Although—there is a pause. I use this pause. I imagine an ordinary agoraphobic-claustrophobic day, a day like any other when I am crouching behind my couch, when my knight in unshining truck might knock only to spot me through the light-admitting window, hiding, abiding, biding my time. That could, under the right circumstances—a nuclear holocaust, an Oz tornadic dementia—be explicable. Without the right circumstances, and augmenting the circumstantial evidence with nudity and unconventional headgear—an impromptu exegesis of intimacy with one's household furnishings might only add to the confusion. Demeanor is everything. Poise. I opt for interrupted impatience. I yank the door, tornado-whorl away my debutante breeziness. I aim for professionalism. "Yes?"

His brown trousers crease. He can't look me in the envelope.

"I just wondered," he says. "We seem to have so much

in common."

"Yes?" I say, adjusting the peak of the envelope on my head, hoping that it looks official.

"Would you have dinner with me sometime?"

"Yes," I say. And shut the door. It rings like a steel plate.

"Sometime" is iffy. This week I have been working on an analysis of Schopenhauer, editing an analysis of Schopenhauer, editing an analysis of Schopenhauer's theory redacted for a chapter in a philosophy textbook. Schopenhauer. Rhymes with shower. Lack of power. Why doesn't he call? Not a tough question. But I miss my clubbiness. Maybe I should order another book? Then *sometime* could be real time.

I scrub the toile upholstery. I spray it with Scotchguard. You never know when *that* might happen again.

I cavil with Schopenhauer. "Conceptions and abstractions which do not ultimately refer to perceptions are like paths in the woods that end without leading out of it." Love, what about love, Arthur? Love, you nasty old reprobate, you misogynist, you canal leaper, you pusher of women down stairs? Surely love could exist in a world of ideas. Love, my noumenon. A priori, fixed and still. My donnée. Couldn't love preexist without having to attach itself to the phenomena of people. I'll stay in the woods, thank you very much, let others seek the trod path out.

But, but. . . . Where is my Mr. UPS?

Will, Schopenhauer, will? Will someone to love you. Will that.

Quietism? I have plenty of that. But no quiet. How

to still the eternal internal dinning? I keep replaying our parting scene. Me, in manila. Him, in brown. Me, saying yes. Him, asking me out to dinner.

"Time, causality, and space are nothing more than functions of the brain."

Might I then, A.S., rewind time, replay the scene? Recast myself as the merchant of Venus, a soliloquy tripping from my tongue?

I am a woman. Hath not a woman chutzpah, toile, dementia, sentences, afflictions, fashions, fed up with the same fools, hurt by the same demons, subject to the same psychoses, healed by the same meds, warmed and chilled by Shelly Winters and Suzanne Somers as a man is: if you pricke us do we not breed?

Yikes. Enough of that. If I could rewind the scene, I'd stop the tape earlier—me, clad; my temples, gray; my head, unenveloped. I'd walk calmly to the door. "Yes? What? Oh thank you. Yes, I'd love to."

How now could he ever forget a woman trying to pass herself off as a naked biped parcel with a home dye job? How could he ever forgive? The quality of mercy is strained.

And then I hear the truck, and I bolt for the closet.

Inevitably, a knock. A knock-knock, and I am the joke. What *am* I doing in the closet? The closet. I have evidently mistaken myself this time for a broom. Emotional Tourette's. I have Emotional Tourette's Syndrome, ETS. I could *use* a steel plate, a patch plate to hold everything together, a stabilizer.

"Kristina? Are you, um, indisposed?"

I crouch with the quiet dustmop, the broom. Oh, sweep me off my feet.

"I forgot to suggest a time for dinner. How about Saturday?"

"That would be fine," I call to the coat hangers.

"What? Sorry, I can't hear you."

"Fine."

"At seven?"

"Yes."

"What?"

"Oh, balls," I yell and come out of the closet, literally speaking. Claustrophobic, you know. Burst out, more precisely.

He stands at the sidelight window. Must have nerves of steel plate, he never flinches.

"Mothballs," I say, waving off invisible moths. "Phew."

He grins. The brown sets off his gleaming teeth and lightning flinders down my spine. "Seven?"

"Lovely. Seven. Lucky number, seven."

He hands me a stack of packages. "I'll pick you up."

I stare into the brown sugar slurry of his eyes. "Mmm."

Saturday. I wear tap pants, one of the Miracle bras, a crushed velvet gown, brown. I confess to immediate disappointment. He shows up in a car, an ordinary car; beige, an ordinary beige; with two ordinary doors, four ordinary wheels. Upholstery, remarkable only for its ordinariness, also beige. I feel wan. The date is over before it begins. Is this some flexion of the cosmic will? Some deterministic means by which I preserve my claustrophobia? Twice, in the car I consider rolling down one of the ordinary windows and leaping out at the observed speed limit. But I will myself to sit tight, to stay the course.

I had anticipated a lark, a joyride in the cunning brown van, mafficking in the traffic, a rollicking, frolicking ride. Sigh.

He drives us to the Panda Palace, along the way, pointing out wayside distractions—his favorite bookstore, antique store. Does he shop for a living?

As he pulls open the door, whiffs of soy waft at me amid a drift of clinking tea cups and ice cubes and convivial laughter. The dining room is alarmingly crowded with happy people. His palm in the small of my back guides me to a table with a centerpiece of tiny paper parasols.

I want to be witty, charming. "Do you, by any chance, have a steel plate in your head?" I ask.

"Beg pardon." He reaches for my hand.

I tuck it into my purse. Staring at my hand tucked into my purse makes me think about muffs, warm furry handmuffs. "I think it's best to get some things straight at the get-go," I say. But I may have said, "gecko." It would unnerve a more neurotic man.

He tosses his forelock. "I agree."

Or maybe I said 'gingko'. "Did I say gingko?" I ask.

He lifts a parasol and hands it to me like a flower. "No, would you like to?"

I cannot look into his eyes. I keep my hand in my purse. "Like to what?" I mumble.

"Whatever you'd like." He lowers the parasol and sets it next to his chopsticks in their paper sleeve of a sleeping bag, twinned, joined. "First dates are awkward," he says.

"And second and third."

He laughs, that brown, yummy little laugh.

I still haven't forgiven him for the car. "Look, why are we here?" I ask.

"I like Chinese. Don't you. . . ."

"No, why are we here?"

"Oh." He settles back in his banquette. "Well, Aquinas argued the primum mobile, and that if we can conceive of perfection, then some ideal must exist. Of course, a leap of faith is requisite for happiness."

"No. Why did you ask me out? I mean, there I was. Naked. I had an envelope on my head. I mean, are you sick or what?"

Both of his hands are on the red tabletop. "I thought that you looked pretty," he says. "I admit the envelope was an odd choice, a fashion risk, but you wore it well. And you order so many books. I am quite a reader myself, and you just don't meet many women up here who read that much."

Is he stoic? Stupid? Stable? I rattle my hand around in my purse feeling lipstick, wallet, comb, the comfortable touch of familiar objects that are not mere projections of perception. Try combing your wind-tossed hair with a perception. I have Schopenhauer on the brain. "You didn't find me 'undersized, narrow-shouldered, broad-hipped, and short-legged' ?"

He shakes his head, that stallion tress whipping. Neigh.

"Sexus sequior?" I ask.

"I found you, I find you," he corrects himself, "lovely, albeit eccentric."

Schopenhauer, I am thinking. Rhymes with Eisenhower which reminds me of a knock-knock joke. "I's an hour late for lunch," I say.

He only smiles and orders a poo-poo platter for two from a hovering waiter.

"I read somewhere that Carl Jung invented the fortune cookie," I say. "Can you imagine that? You crack open your cookie and read the little banner—Where there is love, there is no will to power; where there is will to power, there is no love."

"I would very much like to hold your hand," he says.

I leave my hand in my bag. "Muff," I say, but I may have said 'mush.' Just as well. Or 'much.' I was nervous. "Did I say 'much'?" I ask.

"Not enough. Carl," he says.

"What?"

"Carl. That's my name. Also. Like Jung. I thought you might like to know. And David Jung invented the fortune cookie; he gave them to the dispossessed on the streets of L.A. in the twenties."

Carl. And I give him my hand.

"You are lovely, he says.

"Poo poo," I say as the platter arrives.

It is Sunday, and I am reading Schopenhauer. "A man cannot resolve to be this or that, nor can he become other than he is, but he is once and for all, and he knows in the course of his experience what he is."

Was personality pathology? Why had I behaved so perversely? As Carl had eaten his delicate wings, a spot of grease, just a touch, on the plump soft bottom lip, I imagined going to bed with him, imagined that he was the sort who, when aroused, would roll toward me and say something unforgivable like, "Special delivery for Ms. Corkery. Handle with care." And beyond that. I saw myself calling him after the weekend, only to discover that he answered the phone by saying, "Yello." Not the color. But the telephone greeting that fans of Barry Manilow left on their answering machines because it sounded slick. And beyond that—to discover that he called his girlfriends pet names like "foxy thang." No, no, it would not do.

I needed a tracking code for my imagination. It got so far out there that it just got lost. In the midst of all this and dinner, I tried to crack my fortune cookie open and it exploded crumbs all over the two of us. "Eating disorder," I mumbled; then I turned to him in an agoraphobic spasm and said, "Listen, I really have to get out of here. It's getting way too crowded. Please take me home."

Is change impossible? Do I set out to sabotage every possible love, because. . . .

"Good morning, Kristina," he says then, still smelling of sheets and a hint of chocolate—rich, sweet, secretive. He kisses the back of my neck.

I flick off my computer and twist to kiss his brow. "Git," I say. "Scat. Get your ass back into bed. I am bringing you breakfast in the boudoir." And I hear the espresso pot blow and splatter in the kitchen.

"Go on." And he obliges.

Sour Schopenhauer was wrong. Forgive the liberal translation. Anus obit. The asshole died, his pessimism, grave.

Last night, I asked Carl to take me home, and he did. I found a use for the tap pants. And he never, not once, said anything remotely like, "special delivery."

Carl is taking me for a ride in his truck today, and I'm bringing him breakfast in bed, an almond biscotti, a fortune cookie, apple Brown Betty, espresso with sifted chocolate arranged on a steel plate.

What can I say? Even last night, despite my hunt-and-peccadilloes, he saw in me something—how did he put it?—not noumenal but numinous. Luminous.

My brown bear is moving in. Truth: it was more than just a metaphysical attraction. (The rat-a-tap tap pants.) But it was that, too. There's no explaining the metaphysics of love and no physic for it. It's hope. Faith. Taking that running leap. The lovers' leap, the lovers' leap of faith. We fling ourselves off the precipice. We catch each other on the way down. It's a very optimistic enterprise, love. And everything's looking UP.

The Wig

WHEN MOLLY, MY FIRST WIFE, bought the wig, I was initially put off. A natural beauty, she had never struck me as a wig-wearer. Her hair bounced, short, curly and red. "It's for the beach," she said. "When my hair's wet, I won't have to fidget with it. I'll just put this on." Wearing the wig on her fist, she stroked the long hair that sleeked down her forearm like a pelt.

I shrugged. "Hair dries."

"But I won't have to bother with it. It'll be more efficient, traveling." Molly packed the wig carefully in a hatbox for the trip.

I'd always wanted to go to Greece, and we'd arranged an exchange with a British Classics professor who was also on sabbatical for the year, granting him the use of our Cambridge townhouse for three weeks in his Páros rental.

Leaving Boston during a miserable April drizzle, we arrived to Greek sun, reaching Parikia by ferry from Naxos. The surprising green waterfront drew its clean line beneath the shimmery white buildings of the village. Her hair crimped into tight curls by the salt air,

Molly squinted, her eyes shaded by her hand. "There are supposed to be two great churches—one's on the waterfront. The other one, Our Lady of the Hundred Gates, is famous for its ikons. But I don't think you can see it from here. It has a blue dome."

I shrugged, seeing only the blue dome of sky, the azure strangeness of the sea, the white village aquiver, suspended in light like a mirage. Molly was chattering about the marble quarries, about Asklipiion, the ruins, the churches. But my pagan self had not crossed over for the bound treasures of books, for tour-guided pages of architecture and Cycladean statuary. Leaving the books to Boston, I had crossed for less studied expeditions into the imagined groves of light and taste, figs and dusty sun-split olives, fluttery poppy-reds. "What is the ikon for pure pleasure?" I asked.

Molly squinched her nose, tossed her tight red curls. "Philistine," she said. And she scouted the landing for the red-shirted contact our landlord had appointed to transport us.

When I entered our small white farmhouse, I settled immediately into it, loving its coolness, and shadows, and shuttered windows open to the flower-tangled porch. For the first few days, the wig sat on its Styrofoam stand on the rough plank table by the door. I tried to cajole Molly into walking down to the beach with me, but she refused. "I'm not going swimming at a nude beach."

So I packed a couple of token books and went down alone. I didn't read. I watched the young local girls with their black, coily hair and nearly black bodies as they shyly glanced at the newcomer and giggled. I wasn't ogling. Their nakedness to the sun, their only cover, the crotch hair shaved in decorative vees, simply gladdened me. I turtled into the sand, and threw my arms wide to the sky. I let the heat steam me, the waves rock me. I felt less tired of myself than I had felt in years. In this light, middle age no longer unfolded like a death sentence.

In the afternoon, I climbed back up to our house and ate warm tomatoes and olives on oiled bread with Molly on the porch, sipped the dark sweet local wine. As Molly undressed for bed on the third night, her body glimmered in the cave-like darkness, her paleness, phosphorescent. In the dim interior, only the white wig stand and Molly gleamed.

"Come to the beach with me tomorrow," I said. "It's crazy not to enjoy the sun. We're here for such a short time."

My skin tight with salt and sun fitted me. The sheets whispered against me like fanned air. Wanting her to share this sensual contentment, I slid my hand between Molly's legs and coaxed, "Come with me tomorrow. If you're uncomfortable about it, put on a swimsuit. Just come with me."

In the morning, Molly agreed to chance the beach. I tried not to gasp when she came out to join me with a cheery, "Ready." She wore a demure plaid two-piece, tennis shoes, a towel around her neck, sunglasses. But what stunned me was the wig. Its severe bangs, its starkness, those black as licorice whips on her corpse-white shoulders. I covered my reaction, but she looked like a vampire beatnik who'd holed up in a dim coffeehouse for a decade. Her strangeness hurt me, so I held her hand tight against my waist as we walked to the beach.

The dark girls tittered, but Molly, secure behind her

sunglasses, seemed oblivious. "It's beautiful here," she said.

I told her I was happy she'd come. And with her stretched to the sun on the white towel beside me, I was. She placed her white hand on my naked hip. "Unhook my bra," she asked. And I did, pleased to see her back bare to the light. When she rolled over, she surprised me by slipping off her top. I squinted sidelong at her small breasts, those nipples which my nighttime hands knew so well poked up so alert, so curious in the sun that they seemed alien to me. I didn't dare say anything. Molly only said, "This feels nice." And she rolled the bottom of the suit down an inch or two below her navel to savor more sun.

By the afternoon of the following day, the bottoms had joined the bra in the beach bag. Molly turned a sienna brown that reminded me of our northern Indian summers, of early September oak leaves. Walking naked on the beach, her long body, brown but foreign among the hard black bodies of the local girls, she stood out, but beautifully. She still wore the wig, but now, against her chestnut skin, it slicked long and elegant down her arms, emphasizing her height, or perhaps, like a heliotrope, she actually inched, lengthening toward the sun. The wig's black bangs frizzed into curls from the salt, glamorous and dangerous. She developed an aloofness, a 40's movie star pose as she reclined on the beach among those darker bodies talking in their shadowy language of sounds and gestures.

I got to know the names of two of the laughing girls, Irini and Maria, whose inquisitiveness daily edged them closer to our beach towels. Our conversations were exchanges of pointed fingers, words, and giggles. "Wife," I said pointing at Molly. And Irini and Maria hid their mouths behind their hands.

When we returned in the afternoons, Molly removed her wig and fluffed out her red curls. While I napped or read inside, she sunned herself by the arbor. When my drowsy eyes fluttered open, the wig startled me. Jolted, I'd momentarily think someone was sitting there. By turns, it seemed stately like a marble bust, or ghastly like a decapitated head. I half-expected it to start speaking to me, "Jason, I have returned from the netherworld to deliver you a message." But after an initial uneasy acquaintanceship, I habituated to the wig's presence as one might to an eccentric aunt.

After my naps, I sat on the porch and read. From time to time, I glanced at Molly, enjoying her skin, her browning breasts and buttocks as one enjoys a piece of fruit ripening on the windowsill, a plum purpling to the perfect moment when, neither soft nor firm, it pops, punctured by patient teeth.

Some afternoons, the neighboring farmer wheeled by in his wagon, each day reining his donkey closer to Molly who, pretending not to notice him, rolled shyly onto her stomach as he passed. After a few days of cutting nearer and nearer to Molly's modestly turned back, he reached into the wagon bed and chucked a tomato, splat, between her shoulder blades. Startled, she sat up, clutching her towel to her breasts, her red hair a snarl of light as the farmer drove on laughing and waving at me where I sat, my spread-eagled book unread on my lap. As Molly stared at the farmer's departing back, I laughed too. I couldn't blame the man for wanting to enjoy Molly's nakedness as I myself had. But Molly fixed me with an expression I couldn't read at the time—the fixed stare of a stone goddess.

The afternoon after the hurled tomato, I flagged the farmer over and by gestures offered him some of our lunch. Molly, trim in an awning striped sundress I loved, sliced tomatoes and listened while I tried to converse with the farmer. "Jason," I pointed at myself. "Molly." I put my arm around her and said, "Wife." He nodded.

He spoke a bit of English, knew the professor who annually rented the farmhouse. I pointed at a small nearby island and asked, "What's there?"

He pushed back the white shock of hair which swung over his squinted forehead. His whole face frowned, brown sun-blistered paint, as he puzzled out the meaning of my question, then smiled. "Antiparos."

"Antiparos," I repeated. "What's there?"

"Island," he said, his creased face relaxing as he found the word.

"Island," I said, "but what's there?"

His face ruffled again like a rain-soaked, doorstep-*Globe* at home.

Molly paused, tomato knife in midair. "Antiparos. Antiparos is famous for caves."

"Caves," the farmer repeated, his brow easing.

"Is it populated?" I asked.

The farmer's face crinkled again.

Molly reframed the question. "Do people live there?"

"Ah," the farmer said, his smile an over-ripened tomato slitting its skin, "little people."

"Little people live there?" I asked.

And he nodded, dusted another tomato off on his

pants leg and bit into it, the red juice squirting onto his fingers.

I'm a small man, and the idea seized me. I turned to Molly. My face must have radiated possibility. I said, "An island of little cave-dwellers, Moll," imagining Lilliput or Munchkinland.

Molly bubbled with laughter, and the old man looked at her, perplexed.

"He means few, few people live there," she translated.

I slapped my forehead, then started laughing. The farmer wiped his hands on his pants, stared questioningly at Molly, at me, and then threw up his hands and joined us in laughing purely for the pleasure of it.

Why on that small island in April, when the world seemed so simple, did anything imaginable seem possible?

The farmer hugged us and left. That night, Molly and I decided to go into the village for a drink. Pre-Easter, the tourists hadn't yet inundated the village; many of the seasonal businesses were closed, but a restaurant just outside Parikia, our landlord had advised me, would be open. Still damp from the bath, Molly squirmed into her red and white striped dress and pinned the wig into her hair.

When we entered the restaurant, I recognized the farmer and waved. But he only nodded and turned back to his drink, and I wondered if I'd offended him somehow during the afternoon. I spotted Irini and Maria and waved at them, too. But the farmer muttered something to them, and they averted their eyes. I shrugged at Molly and ordered Ouzo from a waiter who dropped the bottle onto the table with a glare and a snap of his white towel.

Molly's eyes widened. She crouched beneath her black drapes. "Maybe we should get out of here. Maybe it's a local place. I get the feeling they don't like tourists."

I poured the Ouzo. "We're not bothering anybody. I don't see why we can't enjoy our drinks." But we drank silently as stares and murmurs skirted our table.

His hands splayed on the tabletop, the farmer spouted angrily. Irini and Maria huddled near him, talking, Irini's hand placating his forearm, Maria, shaking her head, no. Then Irini, followed by Maria hesitantly approached our table. Irini stared, then pointed. "Wife?" she asked. She pulled at her snaky curls, then pointed toward the farmer.

"God. The wig," I said to Molly. "They think I have two wives."

I nodded and held up one finger. "Wife."

Irini grabbed Maria and turned to the bar, index finger extended. "Wife."

A hubbub at the bar pushed the farmer from his chair, and he crossed to our table, his hands whirling around his head as he posed several questions, all unintelligible.

Irini patted Molly's head, and the wig shifted.

"Take it off," I said.

"I'll be a mess," Molly said.

"But they've never seen one. Take it off."

"Please. No." Molly's eyes glittered at me from the dark curtains. "Please."

"Please," I said. "You'll look fine. You always do. You're a beautiful thing."

Irini clapped her palms together. Molly's eyes flashed, but she raised her hands. Blushing, she unpinned the wig to a loud "ah" from the bar. She rearranged her hair as the farmer grabbed the wig and planted it askew on his head, gesturing open-handed to himself as he jigged. Chairs banged to the floor. The wig hopped from head to head. The room roiled with laughter, whistles. "Wife," Irini said, pointing at herself, the wig tangling in her unruly hair. Bottles of Ouzo appeared on the table. Arms clamped around my shoulders. When some good-natured villager finally nudged Molly and me out the door, my arm was around her waist, her wig was dangling from my pants pocket.

Back in the darkness of our farmhouse, Molly unzipped her dress. It slid slowly from her shoulders, down her hips. Naked, just a shade paler than the night, she ran her hands over her stomach and breasts, then started unbuttoning my shirt. Her hand darted into my pocket and grabbed the wig. She pinned it on, laughing, her raised arms lifting her breasts. She possessed her beauty completely, strangely as she played with the hair on her shoulders. Then she placed her palms on my chest and pushed me back onto the bed. Straddling me, she lowered herself onto my mouth and shuddered. I sucked her. I bit her, and then she slicked herself down my chest, my stomach. She lowered my trousers, and rocked herself onto me, a singsong gasp, as her long hair swished back and forth over my chest. And as she threw her head back, neck arched in moonlight, face eclipsed, I wondered who she was and gave myself over to her hands as she reached behind, under her legs, stroking, squeezing as her dark body pumped up and down.

The following afternoon I sat on the porch while Molly sunned herself. I kept trying to read, but the pages made no sense to me through the anise-flavored fog of the previous night. My eyes slid down the curve of Molly's brown back, mounded the cleft rounds. I set aside the book and walked to her, licked her left shoulder.

"What?" she asked, turning.

And I took her hand and placed it on the crotch of my pants. "Come inside," I said, and I raised her to her feet.

As she turned down the sheet, she smiled at me over her shoulder.

"Put on the wig," I whispered.

"What?"

I yanked the wig from its stand and said, "Put on the wig."

Taking the wig from me, she searched my face. She pinned the wig on, its blackness making her eyes unnaturally large. She slid into the bed and pulled the covers to her chin. I stretched next to her and tried to ease her onto my chest, but her spine stiffened. I parted her legs with my hand, rolled onto her. I remember only that she was very quiet.

During the next week and a half, I was careful only to request the wig occasionally. I wanted back that strangeness, that wildness, but the request hardened her. "Why?" she asked.

"It's exciting," I said.

"Why?" she asked

And I couldn't answer.

When she wore the wig in bed, she did so with all the enthusiasm of a missionary wife accepting her conjugal duty and, afterwards, quickly returned it to the stand. I caught myself staring at it with a fetishistic wistfulness. Snap out of it, I told myself. But I couldn't.

Molly stopped wearing the wig to the beach. When we left the farmhouse, I flashed it a parting glance. It looked lonely for a face. We started going to bed at different hours. When she sunbathed, Molly wore her plaid suit. Her tan developed tan lines.

One afternoon near the end of our stay, I returned from the beach alone and dropped my bag on the floor of the farmhouse. The Styrofoam head, completely bald, stared facelessly at me.

When Molly returned from the village, I asked, "Where's the wig?"

Wordlessly, she disappeared into the door and threw something out at me. It landed in my lap. A mat, it looked obscene, pubic, the long tresses carelessly hacked with a dull knife. I did *not* bury my face in it and weep. And, later, when we discussed it, we both managed to keep our tones even as we lied. She said the wig was uncomfortable, hot. I said I understood, omitting to say that its strangeness excited me, that stranger than making love to a stranger was making love to a strange familiar. But, perhaps, I did not understand that then. I burned the wig in the small open hearth, and, a synthetic, it fizzled quickly to nothing.

We returned to Boston, our luggage lighter, less a hatbox. And I've realized since that our marriage turned on that vacation. Molly could have tolerated an affair with another woman, and, in fact, before the end of our marriage, she did. But she did not forgive me for the wig.

After the divorce, I saw her only once in one of those impossible coincidences that occur only around Christmas and only in New York when and where the odds least favor it. She was standing outside Mary Tully Hall in a lean black coat. She'd let her hair grow long into a pre-Raphaelite tumble of red, redder than I remembered. Perhaps she'd dyed it. She had her arm hooked through her escort's, a tall, elegant man, an opera scarf fluttering over his topcoat. But perhaps I've only added that detail in revision. He looked young, fresh, his cheeks cold-buzzed. I'd heard she'd remarried, but perhaps he was not her husband. He may have been her stepson. I waved at her, and either she didn't recognize me or she didn't notice. Whichever, I felt suddenly foolish and old, a balding stranger estranged from his own past, a lost tourist. I disguised the wave as a flag for a cab, already late for my date, drinks at the Palm Court where I was overdue to meet my second wife.

The Folly of Being Comforted

(for Jay)

CLIFF HAD HAD IT. Since Linda had moved out, there was no one to answer the phone. The phone was always ringing—would he review this book, write that recommendation, play tennis with some emerging novelist—soon to be a minor motion picture. He wasn't getting any of his own work done. Deadline deadzone. He wasn't even getting any of the work done on the commercial book projects. He was huffy, that's what he was, and determined to do something about it. So he called the phone company.

"I would like an unlisted phone," he said.

"Yes, sir. Would you like the forty dollar fee included in your regular monthly billing?"

"Forty dollars? Forty dollars? To not list your phone? Maybe forty to *list* your phone, but to unlist it? Okay, what about this. What if I list the phone but in my uncle's name?"

"There's no fee for that, sir."

"Okay, list the phone under William Butler Yeats." He spelled out the last name.

For the first two weeks after Cliff listed the phone, the

silence stunned him. He had never worked in such glorious quiet. Before Linda, his girlfriend, had moved out, she would answer the phone. But he could still hear the phone ring, Linda speaking in hushed tones, Linda scribbling messages. Now he had silence, splendid silence, to work in. No Linda. No ringing phone. Silence, a writer's paradise. Nonetheless his pet commercial project, The History of Refrigeration, had stalled, so he turned instead to his second project, The Secret Lives of Herbs.

He read what he had written:

Origanum and other herbs cringe at the dreaded cutworm which pupate in mid-summer. The larvae of the owlet moth end their hibernation in the subfusc bowels of the earth only to creep and teem from their foul snuggery to terrorize the roots of the tender herb.

The prose had a turgid horror genre cast to it. Cliff shoved back his chair, rose, made tea, stared out the window at the snow ghosts spuming over the field. He selected his tea with finicky indecision—the orange, no the mint, no the orange. Vitamin C. This time of year, a wise choice, an excellent choice. Now which mug? Not the Shakespeare mug. Too much pressure. Maybe the delicate floral one. He drank his tea. Ten more minutes of aerobic staring. He steeped more tea. Yes, yes, the mint this time for a pick-me-up. The wind was whipping the snow into a flurry fury, bruiting the eddies about like brumal rumors. He let the steam of his tea fog the windowpane, and wrote in it with his index finger, "Ah, the writing life." Through the wet letters he watched the snow skirl.

"Basil, borage, chervil, chive," he chanted. "Potherbs keep old Cliff alive."

He could not bear, he could not fucking bear, to go back to the keyboard. Larva of the Painted Lady Butterfly. Parsley worms. He was a serious poet, for Christ's sake, and a fiction writer. Sweet Cicely, what he had to do to pay the bills. He tried singing out loud, "Sweet Cicely Brown." Actually it didn't feel that odd, singing a parody about herbs out loud. It occurred to him that this might not be a good sign.

It was time to get back to staring out of the window. Yep, mighty cold. Veritable wind chill factory today. Hey, one of those snow ghosts bore a surprising resemblance to Harold Bloom. Or more Zero Mostel? No, Bloom. No, definitely Mostel. Was it too early to uncork that little Vinho Verde from Portugal? A light bright little upstart wine with pretensions but no class anxiety. Three o'clock. If he sipped slowly, it would probably be okay.

When the phone rang, Cliff almost kissed it.

"Yes," he said.

"Mr. Yeets?"

"YEETS? Yeets? You want to speak with Mr. Yeets?"

"Yes, Mr. Yeets, I am calling in behalf of the Tru-brite aluminum siding company. How are you today Mr. Yeets?"

"Appalled, that's how I am. Do you know what is wrong with this country? Do you?"

"You can improve the appearance and value of your home, Mr. Yeets, with aluminum siding, professionally installed, while at the same time affording your home, your major investment, additional protection from the weather."

"Do you know who you are talking to? You can't sell

me aluminum siding. I am a major poet. I live in a cabin "of clay and wattles made" not waffle irons made. And it's Yeats, not Yeets."

"Yeats? William Butler Yeats?"

"Yes."

"Are you the one who wrote *Sailing to Pandemonium*?"

"Yes, yes."

"We read that in high school."

"Yes, yes, that is mine. 'That is no country for old men,'" Cliff recited.

"Yep, that's it."

"I know that's it. I wrote it. 'Caught in that sensual music all neglect Monuments of aluminum architect.'"

"I can't believe it. William Butler Yeats, the poet. I have to call my English teacher."

She rang off. Cliff rubbed the phone against his cheek. Okay, that was diverting. But no remedy for herbal avoidance.

Aluminum saleswoman, what a dilly. Where there's a dill, there's a way. Lovage conquers all. Lovage makes the world go round. The herb book earned the pennyroyal. Here today and tarragon tomorrow. Cliff slumped into the desk chair.

He wrote, "The heinous Japanese beetle performs karaoke versions of 'All You Need Is Love' until lemon balm wilts and flags and dies a slow arduous death." Sigh. Winter in Vermont. Snow packed up around the psyche. Invisible snow lizards squiggled through the brain. Day was two hours long. And too long. Maybe he should make a little plate of Ethan Frome fromage and think about that Vinho Verde again. The phone zinged him as if it were wired into his spine. He jingled. He jangled. He sprang from the chair.

"Yes?"

"Mr. Yeats?"

"Yes."

"My teacher says that you're dead."

"I'm not dead."

"She says that you died in 1939."

"You can hear me, right? Do I sound dead? BOO. Shoo. Old clothes upon old sticks to scare a bird."

"You wrote that, too?"

"I did."

"Look, do you want to buy aluminum siding?"

"Pour moi? Nope. That is no country for aluminum. Grecian goldsmiths made my home of hammered gold and gold enamelling."

"Mister Yeats, it isn't very nice to make fun of someone who's just trying to earn a living. We work for commission, you know."

"Me, too. Want to buy a poem?"

Click.

Okay, in some dim way Cliff hated himself. Okay, she wasn't a member of the gifted and talented class. But he was sick of himself, sick of his meanness, sick of herbs, sick of how he thought. How does one stop thinking how one thinks? He was a total bore, a tidal bore, a wild boar, wild borage. He drank the bottle of Vinho Verde.

Night didn't fall; it fucking plummeted. He stared out the window looking for Zero Mostel, the Mostel of *The Producers* , but he could only see himself reflected. He glared at his shlubby self, body like sausage shoveled into one of those cheap plastic boots you can buy in dismal dimestores. Dimestores? There were no dimestores. His infrastucture was collapsing. He'd lost a briar patch of hair since Linda had moved out. Linda. Bad move to start thinking about Linda, Brer Cliff. He needed to get a dog, something cute and kissy, a Yorkie maybe, a smoochy pooch. He glared at the old man reflected in the window. He raised the empty bottle. "I lift the glass to my mouth. I look at you, and I sigh."

The phone rang. Cliff dropped the bottle. It rolled neatly under the desk.

"Yes? Yeats here."

"You died in 1939."

"In 1942, Zero Mostel debuted at the Café Society."

"You are not William Butler Yeats, Mr. Yeats."

"I am quite sure that I am. I looked myself up in the phone book just last week. And when I called, I answered."

"What was your mother's name?"

"Mom. Tell me what you look like?"

"I beg your pardon."

"Describe yourself."

"Why?"

"Because I dream of a Ledean body." Cliff sat in the desk chair and twirled it slowly around.

"You have no scruples."

"Oh, I don't know. I have one scruple," Cliff said, "maybe a couple of scruples. Scruple, scruple. Have you ever been scrupled?"

"I am sorry, Mr. Yeats, but this is making me uncomfortable."

"How about your name then, just your name?"

"Maude. Maude Gonne."

Click.

The girl was doing her homework. He definitely needed to get the phone re-listed in his own name.

Cliff glared at the monitor. He had pests covered, and was moving on to compost. *Hastening Decomposition.* Cheery thought. Linda had hastily decomposed and been discomposed. The oil man of all things. Of course in Vermont in the winter an oil man was a man of some stature. Slick pumper. An oil man had clout with the frozen few. Cliff could overlook the oil man. But then he found out about the snowmaker. The snowmakers were a weird breed, living in the night, encased in ice, frosted with hoar, they trod the ski areas suffering hyperthermal delusions that they were Thor, the winter sports god of thunder, protector of humanity. Cliff had had it when he found one of these snowmakers on his porch, grinning like he'd just invented wood. The oil man, the Valhallan snowman. Talk about the second coming. He started regarding Linda as if she were a bowling shoe. Something that a demographic map of people had shoved their feet into for a lace up. And when he glanced around the alley, the people were sweaty and smelly and had I.Q.'s commensurate to their shoe sizes. Linda didn't like the bowling shoe expression on his face, so she moved on. New frame.

Decomposition. Can one decompose a poem? Decompose love? Toss Linda on top of the coffee grounds and orange rinds and eggshells?

Shit, I have to concentrate. Staring time. Cliff rose

and peered out the window. Less wind today. The snow ghosts had danced away to fiddle on a roof somewhere. Ten a.m.. Was it too early to crack open that bottle of Sauvignon Blanc, a droll little white from New Zealand, dry but not aloof. Ten in the morning, just an eentsy bit too early.

He really must get back to work on the herb project. I shallot be sage and attack the project. This thyme, I will Burnet up the keyboard. But first he needed to buy a dog. Cliff grabbed his bomber jacket and torpedoed out the door.

Cliff shuffled through the snow on Maple Street to the pet store, Animal Magnetism. The clerk stood with his back toward the door before a tank of Angelfish, whispering to a wispy looking blonde in a trim black coat.

Shit. Linda. Cliff stared. The clerk curved over her as if he were about to slurp her down through a straw like a cherry coke. Cliff felt his face go slack and secondhand, all bowling shoe.

"The lady will have the boa constrictor," he said in a voice that sounded like the cranked up decibels of some enthusiastic over-eager fun-fun-fun soft drink ad for depressives with Tourette's syndrome.

Linda startled, then turned back to the aquarium.

"Sailing to aquarium," Cliff yelled. Why *was* he doing this?

Linda adjusted her coat collar. The clerk whispered in her ear.

"Bowling shoe, bowling shoe, bowling shoe," Cliff yelled. This is what happened when metaphors collapsed, forgot that they were metaphors, when metaphors thought that they were rock stars with addictive personalities and checked into McLean.

"I will be right with you, sir," the clerk said.

Cliff hated him, hated him like one hated divorce lawyers who drove sports cars (it approached magnificent indifference) hated him with his natty mustache and creased trousers. He looked like a waiter in a Van Gogh painting.

"I want a dog," Cliff said. Again with the big voice. The clerk hastened over, looking a little alarmed now, like he was eyeing the phone askance, keeping tabs on it, so that he could make his move, lurch, call 911 and tell them to bring a net before he jumped Cliff and pinned his jugular with a Chihuahua chew toy then hog-tied him with poodle collars till the uniforms showed up.

The clerk pressed his palms together. "You're in luck, sir, because we have dogs. All manner of dogs." He nodded toward the kennels. "What breed are we interested in today?"

"I want a big dog," Cliff said. He suddenly did. He wanted a huge dog, a humongous dog, the world's most enor-fucking-mous dog in the universal pound. "I want a dog big enough to swallow a snowmaker whole."

The clerk tittered. "That *is* a big dog, sir. Follow me, and we will pick out one big dog."

Cliff followed the dapper dogman down the aisle where the dogs crouched under glass like some canine automat. Dachshund on rye. He tramped and stamped as he walked, hoping to force Linda to glance at him, hoping that she would look up and see that he was perfectly okay without her, so okay that he was buying big dogs. Big, bigger, biggest dogs. "That's the one," he said in his over-amplified voice. It bounced off the turtle paradises and fish tanks and ferret cages. It reeled over the hamster wheels. Cliff pointed at a slobbery jowelly weepy-eyed dispirited looking Saint Bernard.

"Excellent choice, sir," the clerk said. "That is most certainly a big dog."

"Want to hear a shaggy dog story?" Jesus, he was ranting now. He couldn't stop. "We had a dog so dumb that it used to sit on one hill every night and bark at the next hill. When the dog on the next hill barked back, he barked again. Haw. Haw. Haw. All night long the imbecile barked at himself. Echolalia. Echolalia. The little peckerhead was using echolocation to tell himself where he was. Like a bat. Did you know that bats migrate? Someone told me this once. I didn't believe him. Where I asked? Where do they migrate? Mexico, he said. Why, I asked. For some quickie Tijuana divorce? If bats migrate, how come I've never seen them, you know, like birds in a chevron, heading south? My friend said, because they fly by night. Haw haw haw."

"Would you like a seat, sir. A glass of water."

Cliff heard the little cat bell tinkle on the door as Linda slipped out to the street.

He went home wearing a restless bomber jacket with a Cairn terrier inside it. Shivering. Thank god he hadn't picked the Saint Bernard.

Four p.m. and already gloaming. Holding the pup at eye level, Cliff inspected the terrier who inspected him.. He set him on the coffee table. What to name the little mange-muffin? Linda? Heh heh. How about Peeve? Hi, I'd like you to meet my pet, Peeve. No, too cute. How about Fergus? "Who goes with Fergus?" Why, Cliff of course, no other. He tried it out. "Fergus," he said. The terrier stared at him. "Fergus," he said again, "Fergus, it is four in the afternoon and time for a libation. Maybe that California Chardonnay, vulgar and cloying, but I'd drink paint remover if it had the right vintage—any." He was not going to fribble at the keyboard tonight.

Cliff popped the cork and poured a saucer for Fergus. "Is there a drinking age for dogs?" he asked. Hell, times seven, in dog years, Fergus could pass.

Cliff tilted the bottle and stared out the window. "Fergus, there is no pun for marjoram." The moon rose full and cut a thin wedge of paler white against the white snow. Small pines dotted the meadow. Sometimes he imagined that they were wee people in camouflage. He swore that they moved, scurrying from one spot to the next in the corner of his eye when he turned his head. Hey, wasn't that one closer? Probably scouting for Linda who had moved into town on Ferry Street two months earlier. One plump tree bore a passing resemblance to Zero Mostel. Zero Mostel sagging with snow, Mostel as snowmaker. In Vermont the snowmaker was the rainmaker. What had Linda been intent on buying at Animal Magnetism, a hamster? A Tarantula? A hairy-legged Tarantula. Linda shaved her legs. In the bathtub. He stared at himself in the black window. Age: three hundred and fifty in dog years. He looked it. Every dogday of it.

"I was not in love with her, Fergus, as I told her many times. She is beautiful, mind you, but intellectually we were not compatible. Linda, I told her, we are not intellectually compatible. Your interests are domestic and familial; mine are artistic and intellectual. It would never work, long term. Then I caught the oil man with his nozzle in her fill-pipe. That is not a metaphor, mind you, Fergus. He was really just filling the pipe, but the way that he looked at her like a new Ferragamo turquoise leather loafer. . . ."

The phone rang.

Fergus hopped off the coffee table.

"Yes."

"Mr. Yeats?"

"Yes, this is Maude Gonne. I am calling to invite you to the wedding. John, John McBride and I are tying the knot, we are."

"Look, Miss, Miss Aluminum Foil, this ceased to be funny a long time ago."

"We're most serious, Mr. Yeats. You needn't be raising a ruction. Perhaps you're in a tippling way at the moment? I could call back."

"No. Do not call back. Look, Miss. Miss, what is your name really? I've had something of a rough day, and. . . ."

"Kathleen Ni Houlihan it is, sir."

"Did Linda put you up to this?" Cliff slammed down the receiver and sank into the couch. He tipped the bottle. "Too much it is, the literary life. It is all simply too much."

Fergus squirmed out from under the couch and watched Cliff roll the empty bottle back and forth with the arch of his argyled foot. "It is just too much, Fergie. How can we tell the caller from the call?"

He rose and crossed to the kitchen and hefted another bottle from the rack without pausing to check the label. He raised the bottle. "Here's to what is past, or passing, or to come."

The phone rang again.

"Yes?"

"Mr. Yeets?"

"Yes?"

"Mr. Yeets have you given any thought to how your loved ones will be provided for should you experience a sudden and unexpected loss of life?"

"Do you know what the problem with the world is? Not enough poetry. People ask me what I do for a living. I say, I am a poet, and they all look at me as if I were vomiting carp onto the canapé tray. So I started telling them, Actually, I am working on a detective novel. *Oh really*? they ask, tilting their champagne flutes against their jaws. *How interesting*. Nobody reads poetry, see, and that is. . . ."

Click.

Cliff and the bottle settled into the sofa and brooded gloomily. Fergus scrambled back up on the coffee table and rested his muzzle on his paws, one eyebrow warily raised. Beyond them, beyond the window, the cold, the snow, the darkness settled comfortably in. Far below them blind tubers bided their time, and tiny roots still frozen in fibrillated curls waited to unfurl. It would thaw. It would always and eventually thaw. They had all the time in the world.

Inside Cliff slurred, "I am going to give Linda a call. Who am I kidding. She's an angel, an angelfish. That's what I am going to do. I am going to ask her to move back in. Think she'll come back, Fergus old boy?"

The phone rang. Cliff lurched. The wine bottle rolled wobbily under the desk.

"Not a chance in hell," Fergus said.

The Writing on the Wall

IT'S 1968 OR 69, and I'm studying cool, Muriel's cool, Muriel, because all the boys treat her to pizza, tease her about being a whore, make jokes about beavers. I am not the sort of girl to whom boys tell beaver jokes. I am apart. I write poetry. I get good grades. I am not the sort of girl. I am not the sort of girl who is always the sort of girl who wants to be the sort of girl to whom boys tell beaver jokes. Muriel will teach me how. Muriel licks at danger like most kids lick at frosting. Muriel's father is a baker. He subscribes to *Playboy*, leaves copies around the living room even when Muriel's home. He laughs too much. He has a way of laughing that sounds like spitting. Muriel hates him. That's why she likes to hang out.

We hang out at J.M. Fields in the record department, watch the tough kids shove 45's into their pants or slide cool LP's into Gomer Pyle Christmas sleeves, the shoplifter's discount. We order cherry-vanilla cokes at the counter. We try on surfer shirts from the boys' department, so they'll be extra tight. When boys try to trip us or tease us, Muriel goes cool, so cool she could freeze a sno-cone solid. She never looks back at them, never giggles, just saunters slow toward the door, filches a can of spray paint from a shelf as she passes. Not a flinch.

Outside the air-conditioned doors, the air flops down like a sponge. The sun is tedious, the trees around the parking lot, listless. I am boring Muriel. She's restless for action which comes through the electric eye—slick hair, bad skin, heading for an overwaxed car. She gives me the tag-along look, and I pretend to be busy staring down some gum on the sole of my sandal. They whisper and laugh and must have reached an agreement, because he takes off. His car is large and loud and slick-black like his hair.

Muriel takes pity on me. "You'll never get a date."

That seems to be a condition of the universe; like day becoming night, it could go unremarked. But Muriel's feeling helpful, aggressively so. She says, "Wait here," ducks back inside, lifts some Yardley cosmetics and a shiny minidress off Mr. Fields, the spray paint can stretching her canary yellow jeans even tighter, the jeans she has to lie down to zip shut, the legs pegged as taut as her skin. Minidress shoved in one pocket, can in the other, and no one even notes her because Muriel moves as smooth as an ice cube melting.

In the parking lot, Muriel draws eyebrows on my eyebrows for me, outlines my lids so I look like a coloring book, and slicks my lips as white as a death-wish kiss, as white and pearly as her own, but I'm still breathing.

"Put this on," she says, snapping the minidress at me.

It's shiny, splashed with lime-green daisies. It feels like car oil in my hands.

"I can't put it on here."

Muriel whips the matching bloomers at me, tugs me by the arm, "Come on," until we're behind J.M. Fields in an alley overgrown with vines, stacked with old tires, wooden skids, cardboard boxes, and heaps of beer bottles, broken glass.

"Here," Muriel says and she unzips my jeans and tugs them down, shakes her head at my day-of-the-week underwear. It's Saturday but I'm wearing the Sunday whites. I suck in my stomach as she slides my jeans off, slips the bloomers on. Then she starts unbuttoning my shirt, makes a dig at my training bra, slides the dress over my head, and squints at me critically, right arm akimbo, palm planted on her hip. She whistles low. "Girl, you look cool."

Then she wads up my old clothes, slamdunks them into a rusted oil drum, turns and starts rattling the paint can, shaking it with a shimmy like it's a maraca. While her back is turned, I retrieve my clothes from the can, fold them flat and pin them under my arm. My mom would kill me if I came home dressed like this. I turn. The back wall of J.M. Fields has more messages than a bulletin board, more literature than our school library: Cathy sucks cock. Larry and Donna TLF. I love Craig Foss. Mona Gordon is a whore. For a lay, call Shelli, 484-3008. Curt has a big one.

Muriel is warming up, twirling her arm, looping big spirals of dayglo orange onto the cement block. She points the can like she's holding a loaded gun. She grins at me from the sheepdog shock of blonde bangs awning her eyes, as she writes in a plump cursive, "For a good time."

"No," I say, but I don't even sound convincing to

myself. I'm laughing too hard. Muriel is giggling slyly. "Going to get you a date she says," then finishes with a flourish, my first name, my phone number there in iridescent tangerine for all the world to see. She punctuates the sentence with an exclamation point, a little orange heart for the dot. The letters are as tall as my younger brother. It's funny, but I'm shaking, too. If my mom ever saw this. I feel dizzy with laughter like we've been sucking helium.

Muriel gives my shoulder a shove. "Don't sweat the small stuff, sister. Nobody ever calls."

For a week, I have trouble falling asleep, think of my mother strolling through the alley, discovering her daughter is a slut. After a week, the worry fades, becomes less specific, just nags me on the brink of sleep like something unfinished, a term paper, an unreturned overdue library book. Then I forget about it; it peels off like flaking paint. I don't think about it until my mom comes into my room on a Friday afternoon, says, "You've got a call." I roll off the bed to take it—probably Muriel—then notice my mother's simpering, knowing expression. "From a boy," she adds in a voice that makes me want to punch her in the stomach.

A boy? I don't get calls from boys. My heart's wandered off, is lost and pounding somewhere in the back of my throat which makes it difficult to say, "Hello." The receiver trembles in my hand.

"This Rachel?" the phone asks.

"Yeah," I say.

"This is Greg." The phone's voice is deep; it sounds like bricks hitting shallow water.

I search the file for Greg. There's a Greg in Earth

Science, but we don't know each other. A Greg in tenth grade, but he dates a cheerleader. I don't know what to say, so I wait.

"I seen your name on the back of Fields."

My head is full of bees. So many bees buzzing that I can't hear his voice.

"What?" I ask.

"I wanted to know if you'd like to meet somewhere, have a good time."

"No," I say. "Yes." My mind's racing like it's gaining on my heart. I don't want to see him, but I don't want my mother to find out. Hive. My mouth races, too. "Meet me at Kay's Drug," I say, "in an hour." Then I think better of it. Kay's is in my neighborhood. He's already got my number; I don't want him to figure out my address, and I do not want my mother to know. "Wait. Let's meet at Mama Leone's. It's across from Fields."

"Okay," he says. "Be there or be square." He hangs up.

I stare at the phone as if it could tell me what to do next. I change my jeans, funnel some change into my hip pocket, and bang down the stairs.

"Where are you going?" my mother calls from the kitchen.

"Out," I yell.

"Wait," she calls back. She ambles down the hall, wiping her hands on her dishrag. She smiles at me with the same twisty smirk she wore when she delivered the Facts of Life speech. Her mouth looks like a bloated lemon peel swimming in the bottom of a highball glass. "Have a date?" she asks.

I realize that I want to kill her. The moment passes. My throat dry, I nod.

"Will you be back for dinner?"

I nod again, fly out the door to avoid my mom's cheery, "Have fun," and I mount my three-speed like some bad movie cowboy eluding an ambush. It's hot. I'm pedaling like a cartoon character, Quickdraw McGraw spinning up momentum. Sweat glues my poorboy jersey to my chest, my back. I'm churning hard, so I don't have to think. But I can't help myself. What if he's a pervert? What if he has a knife? But maybe he's cute. Maybe he'll even like me.

But he'll want to do *it*. Grafitti is no love letter. He'll knock me off the bike and drag me into the bushes and do whatever it is they do and leave me for dead or something worse and close to it and my mom will find out that I'm advertised cheaper than a Gomer Pyle Christmas album at J.M. Fields, cheaper than white frosted lipstick and shiny minidresses, cheaper than free, just a phone call away. Oh god.

And then I'm at Mama Leone's, skidding my bike to a halt and my heart, too, as I scan the place and no one's around—not a dog, not a mailman, not a single pedestrian. I hide my bike behind the building, because I don't want him to think I'm some schoolgirl although I am, of course. And I sit on the grassy median in front of the restaurant and wait, all the time practicing what I'm going to say, finally settling on the truth: my girlfriend wrote it for a joke. I'll explain it with dignity, shake his hand as I say goodbye. He'll want to take me to the Turkey Trot, he'll be so impressed.

Every time a car passes, my head jerks up. But none slows. A few bored teenaged boys whistle as they slink down the street in a Galaxie convertible, but they're just passing time. Like me. A white-haired man in checkered pants smiles at me as he enters the restaurant. A delivery truck comes and goes. The sun teeters on the tops of the cypresses in the cemetery across the street, then dips behind them, tattering them into lace. A chill suffuses my back.

I do not know what I am feeling. No show. Relief? Disappointment? How can I know when I don't even know who called me? But after my panic, how do I explain to myself this following sadness? I watch the cars pass, traffic dwindle, the street lights blink on, one by one, like an illuminating marquee rousing itself to life.

I am not the sort of girl, the sort of girl who boys like. I'd been stood up, stood up by someone who didn't even know that I was bookish, wore my jeans cut too loose, stood up by my first date.

I do not realize as I board my bike and pedal listlessly toward J.M. Fields, I do not realize as I call my mother and tell her that I will be late, I do not realize as I buy a can of black spray paint, as I furtively censor, with sweeping black bars, my name, my number, I do not realize what it will take me many years to realize—that he, too, perhaps was scared, that his heart, too, shook the bars of his ribcage.

I think of him after all these years with fondness, Greg, a boy with a featureless face, fumbling as he laced his sneakers, rubbed the pimples on his chin, trembled beneath his model airplanes bombing him from the ceiling as he, too, skirted his mother's attention, swung out the door, tried to walk at a pace he hoped would make him look careless, but his carefully chosen shirt was dying itself dark with sweat, and, before he could stop himself, he found his sneakers leading him down a side path, pulling him along to the baseball diamond where he hooked up with some friends who helped him to forget his cowardice, his call, his intended destination as the balls thocked into their mitts with a safe pop and they called each other "homos" and "retards" with reassuring familiarity and affection, glad to be boys. The softballs in their mitts and all right with the world.

Greg, forever lost to me. Greg of summer sidewalks, spraypainted in my heart. Greg, a voice like bricks in water. A missed chance. An unseen face. An unbuttoned blouse and unhooked bra. The tremble of the possible. The dream-name I fell asleep to for a year afterward. Why didn't you call back? Was it something I said? Or how I said it? Was it the color of the paint? Now all unwritten, all unsaid. How could I know that you would be my first love?

What It Is

They met at a conference. It doesn't matter what sort of conference. It was a hardware conference, say, at a Holiday Inn. They mingled among the bins of nails, keyhole saws, socket wrenches. He liked the way she hefted her hammer. She liked the way he tested the haft of his chisel against his palm. They were professionals; they knew their tools, their monkey wrenches from their vise grips, their Philips heads from their screwdrivers. The nuts and bolts of life. They introduced themselves. He did exteriors; she did interiors. They lived far apart. As two professional lonely people, they liked that about each other. They could build a bridge to span their solitariness but keep their trestles separate. He thought she looked competent. She thought he looked cute. He liked the cut of her nail apron. She thought his T-bar was cute. They exchanged business cards and half-hearted promises to meet somewhere sometime. Before he headed home, he gave her a copy of his recent manual, *How To Build A Lean-To.*

She read it on the plane. The guy really knew his stuff. His plumb line dropped straight. His corners were true. She thought, hmm.

How to Stop Loving Someone

Courtship in the computer age. A reticulating web of options, electronic avenues: e-mail, voice mail, mail, airmail, answering machines, the overnight expressways to your heart.

She e-mailed a careful compliment: I liked your book, *How To Build A Lean-To*, especially the section on slanted roofs. Your paragraph on gradients and outwitting ice buildup was profound.

He e-mailed back: Thank you.

She e-mailed back: You're welcome. I just re-read the section on ice jams and the life span of the twenty-year shingle. No one else has ever before explored this topic with such sensitivity yet thoroughness.

He e-mailed back: I'm a sensitive guy. And may I say with Excruciating Politeness that I could not help but notice that you are an architectural gem?

She e-mailed him back with the compliment that he seemed structurally sound himself.

He e-mailed: Thank you. Let's stay in touch.

She e-mailed him an expurgated autobiography of her life to date.

When he received it, he didn't have time to read it thoroughly because he was en route to see his girlfriend, Marla, the computer programmer who was telling him to get with the program or delete. He didn't like ultimata. While Marla sketched out her blueprint for his future, he found himself reflecting on slanted roofs, ice jams losing their grip and sheeting to the ground in glorious January sun. It *was* a good section, he realized. It was in fact profound.

She sent him a carefully selected card, a carefully etched Escher print that played with the architecture of perspective. The woman pins laundry. The man stares above the terraced hill at the sky. They are as alien to each other in the building they cohabit as Hopper figures in separate paintings: *Sunday Morning. Gas*. Marine plant life blooms impossibly in a gallery garden.

He sent her a postcard, telling her that his new book, *Building a Snow-fence, Slat by Slat* was out.

She sent him a note thanking him, a carefully selected box of small chocolate hammers, two tins of cookies, and a hand-braided belt. She ordered a copy of his new manual.

He left a message on her answering machine, thanking her.

She left a message on his, inviting him to come visit.

He e-mailed her saying that he couldn't visit now, because he was putting a greenhouse on his garage.

She e-mailed that she was building a hope chest and she'd send him the plans. She sent him the plans.

He called to thank her answering machine.

"Hello," she said.

"Hello," he said. "This is Conroy Cardamom.

"Oh my," she said.

"Oh yes," he said.

They started talking long into the night. They started talking around their short term plans. They told each other stories which featured themselves as heroes. They put on their best faces and forth their best feet. They sketched the blueprints.

Hmm, he thought.

Hmm, she thought.

This guy/gal really likes me.

Hmm, she thought.

Hmm, he thought

This gal/guy is really smart. This guy/gal has great taste in men/women.

She express-mailed him pickled doves' eggs, four leaf clovers, falling stars, mermaid songs in pale pink conch shells, and the completed hope chest.

He sent her a signed copy of, *Your Friend the Retractable Tape Measure* .

She sent him a hand carved trompe l'oeil tablecloth of ormolu. She sent him fudge, butter cookies, ladies fingers. *Feed him, feed him*, she thought.

He wasn't home to receive the package because he was off with Marla, arguing about their future. But when he got home and found the box, he thought: This has gone on long enough. He called her, "I'm coming," he said.

"Finally," she said. "When?"

"Soon."

Soon. Soon is a word with promise, eventuality, rhymes with swoon, spoon, June moons to croon at with a wayward loon on a dune. But that was silly. Snap out of it, her Alpha female said to her Epsilon male. But.

She dreamed of him, alone walking somewhere across a treeless plain. She woke wondering why this man was ambling across her dreams. She woke, singing, *If I were a carpenter and you were a lady*, failing to notice the double conditional. She shored up her empty hours raising high the roof beam, building a bungalow built for two, putting out malt for the rat in the house that Jack built. In between, there was life, interior decoration.

He thought of her occasionally. How *not* to. Why is this woman being so good to me, he wondered. It occurred to him that she was crazy. But, hey, she liked the lean-to, the passage on the longevity of asphalt. She caught on to things. She fed him. Still it might be a pretty trap. Why was she being so nice to him. He got back to work. He bricked the floor of the greenhouse. On Tuesday Marla called and crashed the hard drive. He stared at his monitor, his own impersonal computer. You have mail, it said, and raised the red flag.

"Drive," she said. She sent him a road map, room keys, directions.

Maybe, he thought, possibly. We'll see. He failed to note the red flag. (That is a metaphor.)

As she cut cloth, scalloped it, contemplated window treatments, she sang, "The bear went over the mountain to see what he could see." (That is a song lyric.)

He called her. They exchanged histories, building tips, niceties, anecdotes, favorite movies. She laughed at his halting stories, sly asides. *Feed him*, she thought, *feed him*.

"I think structure is what is important," he said on the phone. "Integrity of building materials. Decor is cosmetics."

Integrity, she thought, we are talking. We are talking. Aretha wailed from the CD player, "But I ain't got Jack."

"Cosmetics?" she asked. They had so much in common. Uncommon much.

He explained his theory of cosmetics. They rang off.

He thought, she gets my jokes. She has a heart as big as the Ritz. He ate all the fudge in a sitting and sank into a sugar low. She erected skyscrapers of meringue and sang into a sugar high, "The handyman can cause he mixes it with love and makes the world taste good." (That is a song lyric and a metaphor.)

How to Stop Loving Someone

She mailed him a meringue of the Empire State Building with a note: I won't scream, King Kong.

He called her. "I don't even remember what you look like."

"Like myself," she, no Fay Wray, said.

"I'm having anxiety attacks of approach avoidance," he said.

"Relax," she said. "Just have fun."

"Fun," he said. "Okay fun. I think if I plan ahead I could find a few days clear."

"I'm afraid," she said. He was scheduling his fun.

"Of what?" he asked.

"Of this." It wasn't fun. "What is this?" she asked as women are wont to do after the fact.

"What is this?" He growled in a gritty blues voice, "Why, darling, what it IS."

She laughed. WHAT it is. She stocked the house with groceries, planted peppermint petunias, aired out the attic, propped his book jacket photo on her dresser, tucked a retractable measuring tape beneath her pillow, baked cakes with flying buttresses, broke the ground, cleared the site, raised a cathedral of hope. In her dreams he was still walking across a vast treeless expanse. (She wasn't receiving the omen.)

This is a bad idea, he told himself. Structurally flawed. Collapsing keystone. Bad foundation work. He jerry-rigged a Tom Swift rocket to the moon.

She e-mailed him: Despite all my kidding around, I really do like you. And I have no expectations.

We'll see: he e-mailed.

We'll see: she e-mailed.

They saw.

He drove, stoned, the tunes cranked, eating up the road, lost his way, recovered, the trip growing longer by the second, the road stretching endless, seven hours. Damn. Lost an hour. She'd be worried sick. Why did they do that, worry? Now what? Cruising, Joan Osborn crooning about God on a bus. Like one of us. Like one of us. The first six hours urgent, then fatigue settling in, numbing his shoulders, the highway elation wearing off. How far away did this damn woman live. Impossible distances to span. What had she said on the phone? Courtship by interstice. Overseas acquaintance by satellite. Make up for lost time. Rolled on the right through the intersection. Uh-oh. Blue light special. Easy now. Pot in the car. He rolled down the window. "Yes, officer?"

She took a bath. She put fresh water in the flower vases. She curled her hair. She changed her clothes three times. She wanted to look nice but not too nice. Lace shirt, too obvious: Come hither. Button-down too prim: Head for the hills. She trimmed the hedges, vacuumed the floors, then paced them. This wouldn't do. This simply would not do. They were both in their forties. This was silly. She took a deep breath. She stared into the mirror. Gadzooks. She looked like Yoda's grandmother. Six o'clock. Seven o'clock. She set out the cheese. Where was he? She rewrapped the cheese. Why didn't he call? They never called. He might be dead somewhere and how would she know. They never called. Anticipation become anxiety become anger become anxiety again. A woman's assonant declension. Then irony: Great, now she'd never get laid again before menopause.

An hour on the side of the road, an hour while the cop

ran the registration. Fucking cops, man. Everyone was doing it, rolling through the intersection on the right. Okay, he broke the law, but everyone was breaking the law. Why should he be singled out for breaking the law. Give a guy a uniform, a big gun, and he's the biggest cock of the walk all right. Officer Dickhead. Gonna get myself a uniform, man, Officer Dickhead meet Officer Anarchy. Blow justice right back into the power-hungry Hitler's beady little eyes. Ka-poom. Ka-poom. "Thank you, Officer," he said, accepting back his license and registration. "Thanks very much."

Gonna cost a freaking fortune. All to see some chick who's a tool groupie. Got to find a phone. Ten o'clock. Cops. Give a guy a uniform and he thinks he pisses testosterone. Cops.

"Thank you officer." Where was the fucking JUSTICE?

He rolled up to a phone booth and dialed in the blue light.

"Hello," she said. "Hi. Thank God. I thought. Yes. How far? Poor thing." She unwrapped the cheese, put a bottle of wine on ice. What room should she be sitting in. Living room, a book, perhaps? No, no. the family room. His manual. Just a half hour now. Eleven o'clock. When she paces in the hall, her reflection startles her. He's here. No, that's me. Where is he? She doesn't hear him arrive. She's in the bathroom, chobbling down antacids.

A knock. And then he was there in the full light of her hall. And she knew the instant that she hugged him that she had failed. He had built her from absence, raised a pre-mortem Taj Mahal from e-mail, letters, doves' eggs. She had failed. And the walls came a-tumbling down.

"Conroy," she tried on his name. Croy, it stuck in her throat. Offer him something, she reprimanded herself. *Feed him, feed him.*

Wo, he thought. This was not the Trojan Helen he'd erected in his imagination over one, two months, two and a half. No, this was what the horse rolled in. He looked the gift horse in the eye. "Hi."

She smiled, pretending not to see the flinch. "Hi. What can I get you? Something to drink? Wine?"

"Fine," he said. He didn't drink wine. No sandpaper would abrade those wrinkles away. No sir. No draw plane either. This girl looked every inch of her long days. Wrinkles, chicken neck. Be polite. The girl has chicken neck. Be polite. He followed her into the kitchen. Prefab mock oak. Lino tile. Trapped, he thought. Trapped like a rat in Kerouac's suburban nightmare of the dream house lit by TV light. Blue beams. Blue light. Thin blue line.

"You tired?" she asked. "You hungry?" Her questions pig-piled. "Wine?" She started heating something up on the stove before he answered. He hated that. Mother bullying.

"Cops," he said. "You should have seen this cop. Fucking police state, man." He looked around furtively for an escape but kept talking.

While he ranted, she stirred the soup. Let him run his course. It was a guy thing. Guys don't handle authority well. This wasn't the greeting she'd anticipated, hoped for. But still he was here. Drove eleven hours. She'd feed him, rub his shoulders. They'd sip wine, talk, recover the easy banter from the phone.

He raved. She set the table. He waved his arms. She poured the wine. He thumped the counter. She served the dinner, smoothed his napkin.

"Here," she said. "Relax. Eat."

Ten minutes. He was here ten minutes and she was already telling him what to do. He smiled and sat down.

They thought, We'll just have to make the best of this.

"Do you want to smoke some pot?" he asked.

They were high. She thought his eyes had gotten bluer since he'd eaten. He liked her crooked smile, he decided.

He impersonated the cop. "May I have your license and registration, urp, please. Would you, urp, while I urp this on the urp?"

She laughed. She fed him cookies, meringue. More soup? Wine? Yes, please, no, please, three bags full, please.

For a giddy moment, they became themselves. They thought that their laughter sounded genuine. They thought they were enjoying themselves, but, but.

She cleaned the kitchen. As she put things away, she was watching herself put things away. Butter in the butter cubby. Napkin in the basket. He was watching her. This was all too much. She was playing into his fear of her: That women always anticipated what men feared: Their domesticity. Which was what they wanted. *Feed me. Feed me.*

"Would you like to listen to this tape?" he asked.

"Yes," she lied. She wanted to run screaming blue murder into the blue moon of Kentucky. She wanted to slit her wrists and watch her blue blood trickle into a bottomless basin. Her nerves twanged like a bluegrass banjo. She was stoned. Neurally jangled. She wanted to talk.

He popped in the tape. Why did women always have

such lousy stereos. He wanted another meringue. Maybe he could just stroll over and puff one nonchalantly into his mouth. He wanted to study her, but every time he tried a surreptitious peep, her green too wide eyes would catch him, appraising his disappointment, judging him for it. He hated that. It was going to be a long weekend. He sat in the easy chair. The arm was loose. Right arm. He listened to her laugh at the tape. She laughed in all the wrong places.

"I love Fireside Theater," she said.

"Firesign," he corrected.

It didn't register. "Remember that one—Don't Touch That Dwarf. Hand me the pliers."

He nodded and stared at her now downcast eyes. What was so interesting about her lap?

She stared at her suddenly old hands. It happened like this when she smoked. She turned twelve, but her hands turned old. Old leaves. Spatulate hands turned over an old leaf.

"Do you want to hear the other side of the tape?" he asked.

"Do you want to go for a walk?" she asked.

He wanted to be agreeable. "Sure." He wasn't.

They stumbled into the frosty air, clopped down the tarmac through the subdivision. He felt that he had squirted like a watermelon seed from his own pinched fingers. The pink pulp of Spielberg's suburbia, sweet watery nothing. Pretentious prefab structures loomed waiting for something ominous to happen, anything, wiggy skeletons to rise jigging from the ground, sentimental aliens to start guzzling Coke. Where was this woman leading him. What was she talking about.

"There's a field," she said, "at the end of the development. An old farm. Baled hay."

He squinted at the pond she indicated with her right hand, but he couldn't see a thing. She shuffled along a dirt road, the way becoming clearer as the development halogens' eerie orange vanished like Kerouac's vision. On the road, off the road, he chanted to himself as he kept pace with her.

"Here," she said. "Isn't this lovely?"

A thatchy field spread gray and rolling open behind a skeletal corncrib. The moon was a perfect quarter, a yellow rocker.

"Yes," he said.

And it was.

"I wanted you to see it." Then she said no more. She turned and walked back along the road. We are talking, she thought.

He followed her, slapped his forehead once. What? What am I doing?

"You must. You must be tired," she said.

"No," he contradicted, then, "actually."

The high was wearing off.

"I'll show you your room." He followed her up the stairs. Her ass was immense. Black leather. Maybe it was just the angle. "Here. Here's the guest room." She indicated the door. He set down his bag. They waited.

"You're welcome. I mean you can. If you want you can stay with me. I mean if you want. You don't have to."

He kicked his suitcase. "What do you think. I mean, I think maybe I should stay here."

"Okay, then. Let me get you some clean towels."

"Thanks." Why do I need towels to stay in the guest bedroom.

She flipped on a light. "Here's the guest bathroom."

He peeped in. "Fine, thanks."

As she slipped into her nightgown, she heard water rushing, gurgling. She wasn't used to hearing water run. Only her own. It comforted her. The toilet seat flapped. The water shushed. Water, water everywhere. She cracked her door. He was there, Conroy. He was smiling. His face looked boyish, friendly.

He looked at her in her yellow nightgown, her face tilted up into the sifted hallway light. Her mouth looked like a forming question. She looked very small to him, her hair unpinned, her back bare. All those freckles. He could play Connect-the-Dots, maybe. He could constellate his own myths, find a quarter cradle of a moon to rock him.

He shuffled. "Thank you for dinner."

"You're welcome. A pleasure."

"You could come down to me. Later. If you want. It's okay." He walked back down the hallway.

"Be there in a jiffy," she called and laughed.

He stripped and crawled into bed, laughing, too. He pulled the bedspread to his neck, upsetting a tumble of pillows. "Doesn't this feel a little weird?" he called.

"Yeah," she called back. "I feel as if I'm in a pension."

He chuckled, letting the down nestle his head, wondering if she would come, nudge him, slip into bed, wondering if she would and if he wanted her there.

Down the hall, she stared out the window, fiercely insomniac. She pretended to read. *The Mystery of Edwin Drood*. I know what he's up to. He is making me decide. That way, he's off the hook. He can say, She started it.

She wanted to whack him one with a hacksaw, tweak his button nose with a plumber's wrench. But did he really expect her to creep down the hall. He didn't want her there. He was being nice. But maybe. Still, why should she. . . . And then she could picture herself not wanting to disturb the moment, the darkness, the surprise of it all, banging into the walls as she fumbled down the hall, stubbing her toe, hollering as she pitched headlong into his shins. Throbbing toe. A choked curse or two. Yeah, that'd be erotic. Nyuk, nyuk, nyuk. Curly does Dallas.

They fell asleep.

She woke first. Maybe it wasn't so bad. Maybe he didn't find her as loathsome as she thought. Maybe. The light spilled into the room, uncertain. Maybe. The morning was pink and yellow. She rose expectant. The sun shimmered between the pointed lace trimming of her curtains. Maybe. As maybe as a butterfly's wings drying, as maybe as their iridescent color, their powdery charm.

So she goes to him. The hall feels very long. She snuggles into bed behind his back.

"MMM, nice," he murmurs.

But it isn't. Something feels off. It is his stomach perhaps. She isn't used to his girth.

He closes his eyes so he won't see her chicken neck. He wants her to be someone else, his old girlfriend Marla who was in her twenties. While he tries to recreate Marla with his hands, she slips out of bed.

They are in the kitchen. He is complaining about the skim milk, only drinks two percent, he says. She says that she'll go out to get him some milk. He starts eating Halloween candy from her freezer. "Please, don't do that," she says.

He glares at her and eats another peanut butter cup.

She wonders why he is doing that. He is overweight.

Chicken neck, he thinks. They all want to be mothers.

She served him some popovers. He ate them.

"I usually have bacon and eggs," he said. She made them.

Why am I doing this, she asked herself. Why am I waiting on this boor? She hated herself. *Feed him. Feed him.*

They spend the day in book stores, CD stores. She knows what he is doing, avoiding her, avoiding talking. So many avenues for communication, but still men and women don't talk to each other. She is growing tired of waiting as he finicks over books and CDs.

When she asks him if he'd like to pick out a movie for that evening, he picks out three. Three. She knows what he is doing; he is finding more ways to avoid her, to keep from talking to her.

She buys sandwiches for a picnic. He is throwing a hissy fit because he can't find ice. Milk, bacon and eggs, ice. She knows two year olds who are more adaptive than this. But she grins. Her face feels tight.

They drive out to the park and sit by the lake. It is a beautiful day, late October Indian summer, drowsy sunshiny day. He wants to climb a trail.

"Okay," she agrees and she follows. Men lead. Women follow. He gets them lost, all the while pontificating about how to keep one's bearings in the woods. She pretends to joke along, but she's had it. He's apparently had it, too. She can feel his strain. She is getting on his nerves. They are lost in the woods, Hansel and Gretel, on a beautiful afternoon, and she feels like a witch. The path dwindles to nothing. He's playing scout, pretending to orient them. She's overdressed. Her sweater sticks to the small of her back.

Jack and Jill went up the hill. The quickest way out is down. "The lake is there." She points. "I'm going down." And she removes her shoes and skis down the steep hill of pine needles.

He follows, laughing, but she knows that he is pissed.

"Impulsive aren't you?" he asks.

"Maybe but I ain't lost."

His eyes hate her. They are full of the dirty tricks he'd like to play on her, saw her chairleg three-quarters through, scatter nails on her garage floor. But she doesn't care; she is skidding down the hill, holding her shoes to her chest and laughing. And Jill came tumbling after. Kit Carson here, can go right to hell. I'm going back to the car. She puts on her shoes at the base of the hill, finds the lakeside trail and starts walking.

He is brooding. It is in the hump of his shoulders. He is sulking. He is not having fun. His mood is her responsibility.

She offers to take him out to dinner. She hates herself for offering. She hates herself for opening herself to be humiliated, to give and give with no expectation of returning affection. But YES, he says, and she buys him dinner. The boy has an appetite. He eats his way through the menu. Afterwards, he says, "Thank you."

It is not, she realizes, sufficient. She pays the bill.

They are lying on the living room floor. She is touching him. He is channel-surfing and trying to annoy her. He is successful. "Would you stop it," she says. "You're driving me crazy."

"No," he says and, "You are driving yourself crazy."

"No, that is driving me crazy. Can't you find a program and stick with it."

He tunes in Tom Hanks in *BIG*. He goes to the freezer and pops a few more peanut butter cups.

"That's what all men really want. A room full of toys, a girl to screw. No responsibility. What a hoot."

He is using the movie to tell her that he doesn't want her. He squirms under her touch, gets up, returns with his vest.

"Would you mend this for me?" he asks. "I popped a button."

And she knows then that she's damned. If she refuses, she is all the bad girlfriends he's ever had. If she obliges, she's his mother. She obliges, cursing. She jabs the needle in and out of the vest with angry little stabs. Damn him, damn him. He brought me his mending. This is over the top. This is the date from hell, but still she sews. She bites the thread off. "Here," she says. He takes the vest. She can't bear it. She pokes him in his jelly belly and says, "Say thank you."

"Thank you," he says and pokes her back.

She pushes him, thinking this is it, the nadir, the pits. Courtship as low comedy. Slapstick love. Pigtails in inkwells. Pinkies in the eye. They look at each other, embarrassed.

"I don't know why I act the way I do sometimes," he says.

She smiles insincerely and he sticks in a video tape, Bergman's *Howl of the Wolf.* They watch it, pretending that they are not watching themselves on the screen. It is not a good date movie. At last, at long last, it ends.

"I'm tired," she says. There are two more tapes. "I'm going to bed."

He doesn't shift. He stares at the television.

Okeydoke. She goes to bed. She wakes up at one. The moon is sifting into the room, shifty light. The hall light is on. She feels the emptiness of the bed. He didn't join her. She rises in her pajamas to turn off the light. The satin makes a shoosh sound as she walks. She hurts; her heart is full of ashes and orange rinds. She wants to cup her hands and find them full. But she comes up empty. In the sudden darkness she leans against the wall.

Pain is pain. Despair is despair. These are not tautologies.

Then she hears her name, and she enters his room, sits down next to him on the bed, brushes the hair back from his forehead. She takes a deep breath to steady herself, because she must say what he will not. "It's okay," she says. "I'm just not your type. I told you that I didn't have any expectations, and that's fine."

"I didn't know," he says. "I didn't know until I came up to bed tonight and I realized that I wanted to sleep alone."

"I knew," she says. "But sometimes it's better just to say it, to get it out there."

"I didn't want to hurt you."

"Sometimes there is less hurt in truth. Chalk it up to lack of chemistry. Too little contact. Too much anticipation. It's fine."

"I feel very close to you now," he said. "Would you hold me?"

She cradles him. Her hands and heart are full. The moon spills into the room. Hansel and Gretel have lost their way. They are two scared children. There's a wolf in the woods and every way, they lose the path. They are hunted by their loneliness. Terror is everywhere. He. She. They, the motherless children.

She kisses his forehead. It is cool. "I'm tired now," she says. "I'm going to bed." She pads down the dark corridor to her room, slips sleeplessly into her bed, and then he is there in her door frame.

"Are you going to sleep here?" he asks.

"That's the general idea."

"May I stay with you? I don't want to sleep alone."

Why, she wonders, why do they only come to us when we leave them. But, yes, she says, her heart is large, her bed, commodious. She suffers from a surfeit of affection for the world and all its sad and lost inhabitants. Come to bed then, child.

And together they lie hand in hand, staving off the night, the wolf beneath the bed, the squalor of loneliness, ulteriority of hope. He. She. We, two. Hansel and Gretel following a path of bird-pecked bread crumbs through the woods. We lose ourselves. We find ourselves again. We build cabins with small thatch. We raise homes in our hearts. We give each other places to abide. You're safe now baby. You're home. For a while.

What is this?

What it is, baby. What it is.

Aground

"COME IN," SHE SAYS without raising her eyes, as if she'd been expecting him. "Hang your oilskins on the peg inside the door."

"Thank you." He peers into the dim room. The cabin smells slick, oily with fish and kerosene. Did she watch him run the trawler aground, he wonders. Did she watch him row ashore? He cannot see the woman's face. She leans over the counter, hidden by a curtain of hair, her arm working a cleaver—chop, chop, chop—across the damage board.

"Leave your boots," she says and points at the bench by the door.

As she turns her head, she parts the drapes of gray hair, pulls them back over her shoulders and twists them together in a single hank, kinking it into a loose knot at the nape of her neck. Even in this sulky light, she looks old. Age has bunched her features. Pouches of skin droop from her lower eyelids. Her nose clumps into a ball. Her lips corrugate. He tries to picture her face when it was young, but the task vexes him. Even in his imagination, he cannot iron out all the wrinkles. She coughs, and he realizes he has stared at her too long.

He glances out the doorway, checks the breeze, his dinghy pulled high, secure on the rocks.

"Behind you. The bench," she says and bends back over the counter.

"Oh, yes." He sits and tries to pry off his right boot with the toe of his left, but it just slides off the heel, well-greased with clam flat muck. He leans over to peel his boots off noting a row beneath him, neatly paired, running the length of the bench. Men's boots, the rubber surfaces crackled from disuse.

Chop, chop, chop. The cleaver hacks across the board. "You fish?" she asks.

"Yes. Just starting out." His right boot yields with a squoosh.

"All men fish sooner or later. My husband, too," she says, chopping, then adds. "I knew you'd go aground there. That sand bar extends further out at mid-tide than people guess. Chart's wrong on two counts. The length of the bar and the name of the island. Chart says, 'Mystic.' But it's 'Missed It,' missed the sand bar. But strange boats rarely do. You'll be all right. It's a coming tide. No ledge out there. Just sand. Soft sand."

"Yes. I was lucky—running aground on sand bottom." He shakes his head at his own stupidity. "This part of the bay's new to me. I usually fish north of here. And when I do cross here, I usually cross to the west. I lashed the steadying sail hard to the shore. 'Mistress,' that's my boat, is pretty forgiving. She should free up as the tide rises." He kicks off his left boot and slumps against the wall. The door is a blinding rectangle of light in the dark room. An oily steam seels the windows. He sniffs. Fish chowder. A pot hangs on a tripod above barely smouldering coals in the fireplace. He searches for small talk. "It's warm," he says. "Indian summer. But it's a fresh breeze out there. Twenty knots, gusty."

She doesn't answer. She scoops up the chunks on the cutting board, crosses to the hearth, carefully sidestepping a rolled pallet, and plops the fish into the suspended kettle.

"Mackerel?" he asks.

"Blues. If you're hungry, help yourself." She nods at a stack of bowls on the counter.

But he doesn't move. It's too hot for chowder. He mumbles, "Thanks," and scans the shimmer of water and sand for Mistress. He shifts on the rough bench. The sparsely furnished room—three rolled pallets, two rockers, a table, a large wardrobe, and some scattered straight back chairs—has been outfitted for function rather than comfort. He wonders when he'll be able to get back under way, tries to calculate the tide, figure whether he'll make his cove before nightfall.

The woman's cleaver cuts the silence.

"Plenty warm," he says again. "But it's a strong Souwesterly out there today. A lot of chop."

The woman only nods.

"Your husband fishing?" He'd noticed no mooring near the island.

The woman shakes her head. "Dead." The cleaver crosses the board with blunt little thunks.

"Dead." He shifts on the bench, murmurs, "I'm sorry," then asks, "Lost at sea?" Under him, the flappy boots slouch against each other and gape.

"No. Just dead." Her voice admits no sorrow.

It is a hard life, he thinks. Scraggles of hair have worked free from her hasty bun. He cannot see her face, but he remembers its lumpiness. She was beaten perhaps. He has known lobstermen like that—rarely at home and, when home, drunk and, when drunk, cruel, their wives quiet and sullen as bruises. No one mourns these men when they die. He studies his feet, picks some lint from his rag wool socks. "You're alone then?" he asks.

"Alone," she repeats. Her voice whets to an edge sharper than the cleaver's. She slaps a filet onto the board. The cleaver drops rhythmically.

"Yours the only house on the island?" He pokes his boots with his foot. They skid forward a few inches, glued together with mud.

She nods. "Only one." She plows the fish chunks to the edge of the board with the cleaver, slaps down another filet.

"Chop, chop, chop." The sound startles him. Not the sound of the cleaver, but a voice. A soft voice. A girl's voice. Only then does he see her sitting on the stool in the corner, half-obscured by the opened door of the wardrobe.

"Chop, chop, chop." Her voice again. Her hand pushes the door aside.

How did he miss her, he wonders. She is the only brightness in the room. Shiny as a jigging lure.

The old woman taps her temple. "Don't mind her," she says. "She's simple."

But he minds her. He gawks. In the shadowy corner of this fish shack with its stingy light and dingy future, sits the most beautiful woman he has ever seen. She is younger than he by a few years, he guesses, perhaps sixteen. Even by this light, her hair, agleam, tumbles to her shoulders, not blonde but impossibly yellow like goldenrods. Her eyes appear gray; in brighter light they might prove blue.

But her eyes hold nothing but their color. Expressionless, they consider him.

"Chop, chop, chop," her mouth says again—her perfect mouth, a mouth he cannot imagine saying "no."" Her skin, undisturbed by the motion of her mouth, glides fluidly. Her face unsettles him—something glimpsed through layers of blue and placid ice beneath which sluggish waters stir—a face of great calm, except it is beyond calm. It is empty.

Her dress is plain, a gray-blue cotton, and reaches almost to her crossed ankles. Her bare feet perch on the rung of the stool. The curl of her pink toes makes him think of small birds—chickadees, titmice. But she stretches long and slender beneath her dress. He can imagine the hollows just inside her hips, the taper of her waist, silky in his salt-chapped hands. He wants to turn away from her; he knows he should turn away from her, but he cannot. His eyes fix, strive to read some response in her face. But there is nothing there. And this he realizes is what transfixes him—that vacancy, the lack of guile in her eyes—offset by her beauty.

His hands yearn to stroke her imperturbable skin. His fingers long to snarl in her yellow, yellow hair, his teeth to bite the plump ring of her mouth. In her gray stare, his eyes swim.

Chop, chop, chop. Not her voice now, but the cleaver's. His neck strains as he turns away from the girl.

"She's not right in the head," the old woman says.

He squirms. He feels as if the old woman is staring at him, but her eyes remain lowered as she talks to the rhythmic accompaniment of the cleaver.

"Born slow. Not much point in sending her off-island

to school. Can't even dress herself." The woman waggles her head slowly from side to side.

He pictures the old woman dressing her, and he has to shut his eyes to keep from trembling at the image of the yellow-haired girl, pearly and naked.

"Her father named her Lily. I never much liked the name. Lee, I call her. It hardly matters. She doesn't answer to names. She doesn't really talk even. Just repeats sounds. So I call my daughter Lee."

He startles at the word "daughter." What magic tricks could time perform that would make this aged woman the mother of this girl? Or had the hardness of this woman's life prematurely aged her? "How did you lose her father?" he asks.

The old woman blurts a short laugh at the question. The laugh rasps, the laugh of someone unaccustomed to laughing. She coughs, recovers. "We didn't lose him." She stresses "lose," shaking her head.

"Chop, chop, chop," says the girl.

He turns toward her voice. Her beauty jolts him. He breathes hard as if he's been thumped on the chest.

Observing the senseless motion of her mouth, his eyes slide down her hair, her shoulders, her arms to the small hands nesting in her lap. Incapable of resistance, he thinks. Fingers as delicate as twigs, fine as straws. Only then does he notice that the joint of her little finger is missing. The finger stubs, blunt just above the knuckle. He thinks of the sweetness of dark rum undercut by the sourness of lemon, the off-note that reminds you that you have an ear for melody.

"Chop, chop. chop." The meaningless words sound like an invitation, a chant. "Chop," she says, "chop."

He rises slowly, pulled by her voice. Forgetting the old woman, he crosses to the girl. He takes her hand, rubs his thumb over the shiny skin of her stumpy finger. He inhales the close lemony tang of her hair. He places his hand under her chin, tilts her head back and stares into the upturned face. He lifts her hair, brushes it back over her shoulders. He feels as if he has been fishing a long time. He cannot remember when he last had a woman. Perhaps many years. Perhaps never. He cannot remember what women at home look like. He thinks all women should look like this girl, this girl he now realizes he has spent a lifetime imagining. He leans over her, lifting her torso toward him.

One chop stops him. The sound travels along his spine. He pivots. The cleaver stands on its own, its tip buried in the cutting board.

"Tide's coming. It comes fast when it comes there in the gut," the woman says. The cabin broods, still and airless. "You should be able to free her now," she adds. She yanks the cleaver from the board and cradles it.

His skin shrivels. The hair on his forearms bristles in animal reflex, tiny antennae transmitting danger. The woman says nothing, but his breath catches on something close to intuition or alarm. The cleaver glints with sharp intelligence, suddenly the most sensate, most conscious presence in the room—keener, more brilliant than yellow hair. Without looking at the girl, he releases her. He feels her weight shift from him as she settles onto the stool.

Time attenuates. A season has turned since the woman last spoke, but only a minute has elapsed. His jaw works woodenly. "Yes. I should get my boots on and get back to the boat."

Watching him, the cleaver gradually lowers itself to the board, lies down on its side.

But he does not turn his back to the blade. He eyes it intermittently as he pulls on his boots. He consciously averts his eyes from the girl, checks Mistress' lie. She's vectored toward deep water, headed up. He stamps his heels. Dry cakes of mud drop from the boots, puff small silty clouds as they land on the floor. He inhales slowly, self-consciously. The history breeding in the oil smells and fish smells of this dark, sad room rises, surface like a body lost at sea. Preternaturally alert, he sees the father, drunk, forcing himself against the girl, threatening his wife that he will kill their child if she interferes. She tries to force herself between her daughter and her husband. And her husband, who is a man who keeps his word, chops off the child's fingertip as a caution to her. Chop. The child screams. The woman waits, endures. When he is done, he passes out on the pallet. She binds the child's finger, listens until sleep mutes the girl's whimpering. While the child sleeps, the cleaver kills him.

The story loops through his mind. He doesn't know why he suddenly knows this story, but he doesn't doubt it. The knowledge is simply there like preliterate knowledge: breathe, suck.

He slaps on his oilskins and stands in the door frame. "Yup, she's floating free. Thank you," he says. But he barely looks behind him at his boat. As he leaves, he never shifts his vision from the cleaver.

Wordlessly, the woman slaps another filet onto the board. As he walks down the bank, he hears the chop, chop, chop diminishing behind him.

But sometimes in the shuttered darkness of his dreams,

the sound grows louder, closer like his heart. He keeps time as it beats, chop, chop, chop, with a yellow-haired girl who sits on a stool. She does not age. Behind her cabin is an unmarked grave. He knows this although he never returns to the island misnamed "Mystic."

He might have earned himself such a grave. For a while, he thinks he's made an easy choice of life over death, survival over lust. But as he's gone farther asea, the choices no longer seem distinct, either one, a desire to preserve his life. Either one might have affirmed him.

Had he been a different man, braver, perhaps, or crueler, he would have a memory now to warm him, a memory of taking the beautiful girl who burns her way nightly into his dreams, a memory cleaving his heart. But he was not that man.

Her father was. Sometimes he considers him. How could a man commit such an act? No answer comes. Some hearts are uncharted.

The yellow-haired girl comes and goes; his days and nights entwine, intermingle sleep and waking. They no longer separate into distinct states. Sea and shore. Sky and sea. Once, rocking in the dream, he rips the gray dress, falls heavily on the naked girl. She disappears beneath him into a gray rag on the floor. When the dream ebbs, he lands, waking to his hips grinding into his bunk tick.

"Missed it." Again he runs aground.

Tide Walk

AT FOUR IN THE MORNING, I walk alone. Even the fishermen are not up yet. The sandbar rediscovers itself in the draining tide, in a world trickly and silvery with phosphorus and moon, tricked out with water and stars. The sandbar extends a path from Great Chebeague Island to Little Chebeague, and it flutters with gull wings, a white tremor in a dim world, the tremor of a gullible heart. At my approach, a rush, a flush and flurry of white. The seagulls betray themselves as they carve ellipses in the sky.

A curve is the shape of a wing is the shape of an unfinished sentence, the silence defining the unspoken word. Rocks emerge from hovering sea fog as all things emerge from their absence. The ledges compose themselves like letters contemplated but never written or mailed, letters written in the solitude of the irrecoverable chance, addressed to the teacher who affected you, the lover who disaffected you.

What motivates a middle-aged woman to rise before her dreams complete themselves, before the day stutters back into its introductory clause? What motivates the pen to write the letters it *does* write?

How to Stop Loving Someone

When you were my mentor, you said the epistolary form is dead. The second person is unmanageable. The apostrophe, you said, is an outmoded device. By apostrophe, I assumed you meant a symbol for what was missing, not an address to an absentee, only to learn later that what is missing is who is missing. For brevity, we punctuate our lives and letters with apostrophes, ellipses. . . .

But first, a story. Douglas Marsh, a man twisted by age into driftwood, sat in the shadowy interior of the Chebeague boatyard he once oversaw, a decoration like the shark jaws pegged to the wall, the oversized lobster claws, prized for their oddity. While he watched his son work, his jaw worked, munching first one anecdote, then another. The stove steamed against the fizzle of sea fog. It was a cold morning, but warm inside, when he said, "Little Chebeague was settled when I was a boy. A whole fishing town there, a cannery, a store. Actually," he revised, "it was unsettling then, when I was a boy. The families were just starting to leave because the cannery was closing. Most of the families took their chances here, relocating to Great Chebeague which had a ferry to the mainland."

I watched Marsh's son consider the damaged daggerboard I'd brought in. "Can it be fixed?" I asked.

He nodded. "Maybe."

"I wasn't watching where I was going," I said, apologizing for running aground.

He turned his face away from me, the repair an imposition, an avertible accident.

Douglas Marsh droned. "Pretty soon nobody lived there. Pier collapsed into the water, pilings rotted. Brush grew up. We island boys used to walk over there and chuck rocks at the windows at low tide." He chuckled. "Later, we tried to coax our girlfriends to walk over with us."

I smiled. "And?" I asked.

Shark-like, he grinned. "Some did. Some didn't."

"How do you walk over?" I asked.

"From the hook." He squinted at me. "You want to be one who did, eh?"

We laughed together. Then he started another story, opening it from its middle like a book with a cracked spine, a story about a rabbit swimming over from Cliff Island, a fox a stroke behind. "I didn't know they could swim," he was saying as his son's finger scolded the ding in my daggerboard, and I reentered the mist beyond the boatyard door.

After hearing the elder Marsh's story, I knew that I wanted to smash windows, that I'd wanted to smash windows my whole life, that I was one of those people who never smashed windows, being either too civilized or too timid. I knew that, sooner or later, I would smash a window, walk at low tide to Little Chebeague and hurl a rock with the pent-up wildness and recklessness of a lifetime.

A walk is not a straight line, but a zigzag through time. Water trickles in rivulets back into the ocean, which bridles, bucking at a distance, near dead low. Everywhere movement but no urgency. A story is not a straight line but a blue and rimless bowl rising to contain the shape that will define it. Ten years intervened between Douglas Marsh's telling of the story and my bare feet slapping across the hard, emerging band of sand. In that interval much happened.

How to Stop Loving Someone

The story teller died. I married the man I'm divorcing. He sold the boat with the damaged daggerboard and bought a bigger boat that drew more water. My son was born. You loved me for a while.

What motivates a woman to rise before her dreams complete themselves, to leave the house as quietly as a folding sleeve so the husband and son she betrays can sleep? To break a window. To displace herself, to wander off like a memory belonging to someone else. To assume the unnamed longing teenaged boys' faces wear as their eyes glimpse an out-of-state license plate passing through their small town.

Gulls etch their circles, sweeping down, again and again, for the blue mussels which they swipe upward to drop to crack upon the rocks, the blue jewel-boxes unhinging, splaying stories begun in the middle, their book spines split. The mussel centers quiver, a life form as simple as a nerve. They open themselves to a squawk, a beaked jab. Perhaps there's an instant, a shiver, when the mussel shrivels into its shell, but no concealing chamber opens to receive the reflex. How quiet endings are after all the commotion.

Gulls skim the draining flats. My feet pad over a road paved with chipped shells, the cobalt blue of mussels, the nacre, the furze of the beard. Little Chebeague grows bigger. As the fog retreats, the day becomes itself. A boat, unseen, chugs. A radio crackles, amplified by water, a static of unindividuated words, atmospheric disruptions. A lone woman, her skirt looped up between her legs, bends rhythmically, scalloping in the shallow waters off the island. As my feet slap up the exposed beach, remnants of the abandoned life, an iron cleat ring, a rusted mangle of machinery, a corroded outlet drain, press their memories through the sand and the high-tide detritus on the shingle. The scalloper wades off toward her anchored pram.

Last month two gestures informed me I would leave my husband. My favorite red sweater packed itself in my overnight bag, intuiting I wouldn't be returning to the summerhouse next year, and anxious not to be left behind. And when the family drifted, mackerel-jigging on the *Loki*, my husband's hand pressed its affection on my shoulder. While my nerves managed to contain the reflex, my soul cringed, shrugging off its touch. After bickering years, shouting doors, love ended with a folded sweater and an undetectable flinch. I'm glad I'm leaving him for me and not for you, but still I wonder, now that we no longer write, what ended it for you, a tilt of my head, the way I drank my iced coffee, never stirring the sugar settled in the punt of the glass? Once when I asked you if you still loved your wife, you said, Love leaves the back door open. Later, you said, Love like a hospital gown opens at the back. And you slipped out.

The sharp-bladed seagrass on the bank paper-cuts my calves. The lines fill with blood. A mosquito whines. I rub my legs and scan the treeline for the peaked roofs Marsh's story raised in my imagination. I scout for a suggestion of a road or path, but see only scrub-growth, hardhack. If there are any houses here, they must be interior, so I follow my chest's thrust into the brush. The scrub yields barely, scratching, thrashing. But after several yards, a way reveals itself, not a path, but a swath where the puckerbrush hunches closer to the ground than the surrounding bushes. Raspberry and blackberry suckers, clumps of daisies, spiking thistles. I follow the lower growth through its twists, water seeking a stream bed. A path is not a straight line.

"Love is not a straight line." That was your line. At dinner parties, you liked to talk of love, diverting the conversation from its natural course through politics and politesse. "Let us talk of love," you said, crossing your fork and knife, hexing all other topics. Your wife, marginal as a footnote, stared at her empty plate. We traveled in the same circles.

The first time you made love to me you said I had a fleeting quality, reflected sunlight, flitting over the walls of an upstairs bedroom. Men are drawn to that fluttery quality, you explained. Men cannot bear *not* to try to catch that restless independence in their hands, to hold it still, to pin it down. Flattered, I didn't realize that you were labeling me, insubstantial. Later, revising, you said, Men and women are not intended to love each other; this is why they keep attempting it. As I felt your love ebbing, I wrote you a letter of recrimination. When I told you about it, you advised me not to mail it. There are only two stories, you, my teacher, said, worth writing and reading: love and death. At the time, I thought they were disparate stories.

My hip bangs into the first house without realizing it. The pain foreshadows a bruise. A stack of wood crouches in the weeds. But then I trace the pitch, note the few fluttering shingles. A roof. Only a roof, no house, no windows. Did the house sink into the clay? Did a storm rip off the roof and gravity place it here? I rub my hip and push on, grass whipping my legs. There must be other houses.

By this afternoon, my son will be in another house. My husband is taking him away from me for the first time. While I must learn to bear the absence, I cannot bear the separating. "Nouns," you said in class, "oppose the activation of a participle, verbs which long to become gerunds." Screaming is a scream, is a rising pitch and a fall. A roof. A love affair. A plot. A life. You between my legs, all a rising pitch and a fall, or some other diagram.

You said the most difficult task posed by love was to convince itself it existed, that after the rising pitch, love wasn't just inertia or habituation. Like a baby doll, you cried real tears. You said you didn't know what love meant, that people assign "love" different meanings. I said love was not a meaning; it conferred meaning; love was a feeling. Have you felt it, you demanded. And I didn't answer. The answer was, Yes. But only once, for certain.

My legs are crusted with blood. I'm grateful not to be home while my husband is packing my son's dinosaur-figured underpants, his blue jeans with the holey knees, his finger-painted tee shirts. I'm grateful to be away from our summer house with the realtor's sign hammered into the lawn. The sun heats me irritably. I doubt the existence of houses here, of windows longing for rocks to obliterate their panes.

But second, a plot. Assume a plot is not a story. A plot has a shape, a guided shape. Assume a story assumes no shape, but reveals itself like life, like a walk on an unknown island, that it encompasses the promise of surprise. Don't confuse story with chronology or action. A story is not a walk revealed step by step, chronologically in time. A plot is only a shape superimposed on a story. Plots construct themselves; stories reveal themselves. I'm following a path that's not a path but might have been a path once, a natural clearing where someone blazed before me.

Assume we are sitting again at the table where, eight years ago before I bore my son, you, after making love to me, were pouring a glass of burgundy for my husband who did not yet know I was going to leave him, that I did not yet know you would leave me. Assume you were talking about love, gesticulating in your buffalo plaid shirt as you knocked over my goblet and my husband rose, amused by your passionate performance, to find the dishrag to sop up your clumsiness. Assume that, even then, I was doubting my long-held belief that love was a hedge against death. Assume that, even then, I knew that love was ineffectual, knew that loving was impossible while we lived, because the self like a rabbit would always stroke a paw ahead of the following fox until the fox, realizing he would drown or eat, would open his jaws and drown. Assume all that; I cannot attest to it. But I can attest to this; I knew love in a moment, and that was not the moment.

The moment I knew love surprised me like the house rising before me now as I walk down a path which is not a path but a natural memory of a past where people, I assume, once beat down a walkway in order to get from here to there, from the fisherman husband arriving home, exhausted with his haul for the day, to these collapsed houses where the fisherman's wife fed him anything but fish, perhaps the steak from the cows who'd dehydrated, lapping up seawater which made them taste like fish. Assume anything. Assume the wedding gown my mother wore which I wore on the day I assumed that my marriage would last fitted me with a bodice beaded with words. Assume my wedding vow ran from me, words seeking a stream bed. Spring water.

When my waters broke, I was still untutored in love. I'd carried the moon in my belly for months, irritated as it tugged my body and moods into unnatural shapes. The labor was long. I was so busy with my pain that I did not recognize my screaming. With a bloody yank the doctor pulled not a moon from me but my son. My hospital gown opened at the front. He placed my son on my chest, and, as the squirmy squalling thing urinated on me, I tried to hug him back inside. I hadn't foreseen feeling this, not this. My legs crusty with blood, I knew love in a moment, rising forever like a blue and rimless bowl to contain the sky.

This morning I realized that it is not the moment of pain which hurts; it's losing the moment of pain which hurts, the pain that can shock you into knowing you're alive. I can't recall the pain of birth. I can only recall that I felt it. I'll never feel it again. Each pain is unique. Even the pain I avoid, the pain of dinosaur-figured underpants stuffed in a suitcase. Love, you said, stubbing your cigarette in the open palm of my hand, is testing what others will endure for you. Your cigarette wasn't lit. You smoked Kools, I think. Details, you advised me, make the story.

The house now stands before me. It has an entrance but no door, windows but no panes. How does one break windows which have no glass? It's badly beaten by weather and time, wood shingles and clapboards stripped here and there, revealing the skeletal structure beneath, barn boards and plaster crumbling through the ribs of lath. Now I know what the summer house does while I'm away. I used to think it ceased to exist, that I resurrected it each spring when I removed the dust shrouds, tossed mothballs in the bin, swept up the mouse sign. What becomes of former lovers? Do they dream of us dreaming of them? Do we wander in like stray thoughts now and then? Once they spill us out of the blue bowl of their preference, do we slide away, cease to be that person whom they've loved? Is it a small death somehow, and between lovers, a limbo, until the next lover, divine, conjures from the void of self some other person whom he needs to love? Will my son think of me while he's away? How often? Will he miss me?

I enter the doorway that has no door, and immediately I know this was once a beautiful house. In spite of the litter, raccoon scat and aluminum cans, the ceilings arch high. The second floor has dropped onto the first like a hasty lover, pressing as close as surfaces allow. The staircase crazily ascends into air. Tentatively, I test the boards, slip my thongs on my feet and crunch across the glass-glittered floor. I peek through a door at a room that is a hill. An etiolated tree roots in the parlor floor. Before you closed it, I thought love was a door without a door. I hadn't yet considered staircases and trees although these, too, might pose possibilities. Only this morning I learned how much can be packed into a departing suitcase. Anything's possible.

I place my hands on a sill of the window and lean out, imagining the air the fisherman's wife inhaled while she planned the evening meal for her husband who'd be returning any minute now. On the floor between my feet I spot something, round, a crinkle of latex. A condom. The fisherman and his wife move out, and someone replaces them. Douglas Marsh, only he is younger than himself, about sixteen, and his shoulder obscures the face of the girl with the silvery giggle who tugs down her blouse beneath him. When he shifts, sliding his hand inside her blouse again, I glimpse her face, and it is a perfect face, softened by youth, a face that doesn't know how young it is. They laugh, tussling as they make love. When he kisses her, I open like her mouth to his tongue. A shaft of sunlight shifts through the unglazed window, and her thighs sparkle with the broken glass embedded there. Her legs part, unhinging like halves of a shell. There's a tentative moment, a moment flashing like light, when she pulls instinctively back, afraid. "No," she says. And she's wringing her skirt in her hands, feeling the island isolating itself with the reversing tide, the water that could enisle her here with the night. "Yes," he coaxes. "Yes," she answers. I shut my eyes. I listen to the dry floorboards drinking the wetness that spills from them, the wood grain swelling. When I open my eyes, the couple has left. A fallen nest unravels in the corner where they lay. And I know by the angle of light that the tide will begin to reverse itself, first in surreptitious trickles, then in a surging swash. I know that I, too, need to be leaving.

I haven't smashed a single window, but the whole world's flooded in. I wish I'd had a minute to tell the beautiful girl that she needed to be wary of that beauty, because everything beautiful is placed here to be broken. Beauty, like a hinged jewel-box, a blue shell, a rimless bowl, begs for carelessness, or cruelty, begs for fracture. But I didn't want to intrude.

At four in the afternoon, I am alone. I toss a shard of glass through a window frame from a house that cannot seal the world outside or in. I close no door behind me. My tide walk, still incomplete. Can you answer me now, my second person? Can you answer this letter I will never mail to you, if love is not a straight line, if love like this sentence is conditional, then . . . if . . . then . . . love . . . then. . . .

Halfbaby

HALFBABY'S ALWAYS BEEN HALFBABY like she came with the name. Maybe the island midwife gave her the name, she doesn't recollect clearly, fully, but she's Halfbaby just like Rockmother is Rockmother. But Rockmother didn't come with her name. The midwife named her Rockmother when Halfbaby was born. Halfbaby thinks it's because she stands up to things like the rocks do on the shore on the weather side of the island. Rockmother's birth name was Ruth. The island people call her Rockmother, though, the name as tight to her as a barnacle. It's a funny name because Rockmother is all lap. She has a lap even when she walks. She has a lap until she sits down; then her flesh settles and her flowered dresses tent down to her ankles, ankles as thick and white as birch trees.

Halfbaby was born here in the house. Some island people go to the mainland to be birthed, but Halfbaby's never been there. She thinks of the mainland like limbo, the place where babies float while they wait to be born. More women go over on the ferry now that the midwife's dead, but not Halfbaby; she stays put.

How to Stop Loving Someone

She lives with Rockmother at the three corners near the back cove, next to the marsh farm where the three sisters live: Poppy, Rose, and Lily. They didn't come with their names; their mother gave them to them a long time ago, before the midwife, before Halfbaby. The sisters' mother loved flowers and the flowers tumble all around the farmhouse in unruly beds now that the sisters forget to weed.

Halfbaby loves the three sisters. They are as old as the umbrella tree on the sandy hook, all in their eighties at least, and they forget things, daily things like weather and eating and where they are and who's dead and alive, but they never forget that they are ladies. They all dress before leaving the house, always hats and gloves, and black button up coats, and the trim little lace-up heels that they store in the attic to cure the leather, to make it last. Halfbaby bets those shoes are in their eighties, too. One of the sisters, Halfbaby's not sure which one, married a Cole boy at the East end of the island, but she got homesick—even though it's only five miles one tip of the island to the other—and moved back to the farm.

Before she moved back, she dropped a son on the Cole boy, and the boy moved in for a while, not too long ago, in Halfbaby's time. Halfbaby isn't sure how old she is; she thinks that she might be twenty, might be thirty, in there somewhere, all the years feel the same, time moving like light and shadow, like tide, like snow, here, then gone. But the Cole boy moved in with the sisters in Halfbaby's time, and he built gates on the doors with latches on the outside to keep the three sisters from wandering out of the farmhouse, to keep the sisters out of his gear.

He wasn't mean. He was trying to protect the sisters, keep them from wandering to places that weren't there any longer. Keep them from that baffled look they got when they arrived at some place that wasn't there with that straggle-haired bewilderment: Where is the store? The farm? Where is the place that I am standing in? Where is the world? What was I about to do, here in this place that isn't here?

He tried to keep them from that. He tried to keep them in place, in time, and out of his tools. He was an electrician.

But you might as well try to keep lightning out of the sky. The sisters just kept getting out, getting tangled up in the coils of wire, banging into the spools. And he gave up. He was a good boy for coming home, but he just gave up. He moved to the mainland, and disappeared as far as Halfbaby knew, disappeared among all the impatient unborn across the bay.

Rockmother didn't like him, but Rockmother doesn't have much use for men anyhow. She says she's more comfortable around the women. When Halfbaby asks her about her father, Rockmother just snorts. She says her father was a rooster and that makes Halfbaby laugh because then Halfbaby would be half rock, half rooster. She can feel the rock in her when she crosses the salt marsh and stands on the shore, feeling the outcrop beneath her feet as she watches the wind whip the whitecaps up like egg whites. But she feels no rooster in her; she's got nothing to crow about. Rockmother tells her that.

The sisters used to keep roosters, hens too, there in the yard. There'd be piles of eggs in the juniper bush, at the base of the elm, surprising places, and the ones the raccoons didn't get would cook in the sun, smell awful if they cracked. But the chickens wandered off, and the sisters didn't miss the eggs. No chickens now. But as Halfbaby squints through the flyspecked glass she thinks that she can still make them out, scratching in the driveway, walking that comical walk like their two ends are headed different ways only to have them bump back in the middle. It makes her laugh as she cracks the egg against the rim of the yellowware bowl, the one with the blue stripe, and Rockmother startles, stares needles at her. "What you laughing at? You gone simple again? People who laugh at nothing, they got places for them."

Limbo. Mainland. A place for people like that. But Halfbaby doesn't turn around. She feels the needles in the back of her neck, but they don't hurt. They stitch time. She thinks that she can hear Rockmother's laps settling comfortably down onto her thighs, unfolding like dough over where her bedrock lap should be. That's what morning sounds like, quiet enough to hear what you cannot see, Rockmother's fat oozing, the yolk dripping out of the shell, the long-gone chickens scratching in the sisters' dirt yard. Halfbaby carries a lot of time in her; she has a gift. She's not simple, but she sees beyond sometimes.

Rockmother wants corn fritters this morning, fritters with maple syrup, and Halfbaby's reaching for the whisk when she sees the twin yolks nestling in the bowl. "Double yolk," she says. "That's good luck. Rose told me double yolks bring double good. It's an omen."

Rockmother grumbles. "I don't know about omens, but we can use the luck."

And Halfbaby cracks the second egg, and that one's double too. Double double. Never seen a triple, no yolks like the three sisters. She doesn't tell Rockmother about the second egg, but she's happy. And she whistles as she scoops some flour in her hands, lets it sift down through her fingers onto the yolks, cozy in the bowl. She heats the fat on the cook stove and listens to Rockmother creak on the rocker with the stubby legs. Rockmother likes that chair because it leans forward to catch her weight, and the legs are short. She can tilt in and out, wait for her body to catch up with her when she raises or lowers herself. She grunts a little as she rocks. Halfbaby drops some water onto the fat to test if it's hot enough. The water spits. She scrapes some corn off last night's ears into the bowl, then spoons the batter into the fat and listens to it hiss as it plumps up, rises as it fries. Rockmother loves breakfast. Halfbaby is always careful with breakfast because she knows that it readies Rockmother for the day. She can be sloppy with lunch, serve leftovers or sandwiches, but breakfast matters. When the fritter is just as gold as August corn, Halfbaby dips the slotted spoon, rescues the fritters. "There," she says, setting the plate, the pretty morning plate, blue depression glass, on the daisy sprinkled oilcloth of the table. She waits for Rockmother's body to shift. "There," she says again and arranges four flitches of bacon neat as star points around the centered fritters, pooling amber in the syrup. Mornings are good.

Halfbaby doesn't eat breakfast, just juice and coffee. Morning food makes her sloggy, like bees are droning in her head. She likes her head clear and light so that she can see time. She's as thin as Rockmother is fat, looks more kin to the three sisters who are spindle thin like cob dolls, than she does to Rockmother.

Mornings, after she cleans the dishes, she likes to sit in the attic. Used to be mornings she had home school with Rockmother, doing figures and letters. Rockmother liked reading the horse hide Bible, where there's a book named for her—not the Book of Rockmother, the Book of Ruth, her name before she hardened. Ruthmother.

Halfbaby liked the reading better than the figures. She never had knack with numbers. She thinks some people think numbers, some think words, or maybe scenes. The Cole boy used to think numbers, maybe he still did over on the mainland, counting like he used to do here: I been to the mainland twenty-two times this year. That spool's got a good four yards yet. Takes twenty minutes to walk to the pier, twenty-four in snow.

He knew degrees Fahrenheit, the pound weight and ages of people he talked about, their shoe sizes, how many lamp posts and mail boxes lined the back cove road. He must have spent his whole life counting. When he talked to Halfbaby, his numbers made her dizzy. They cluttered her up.

The attic clutter didn't make her dizzy. She knew everything that was there even if she didn't count it up. From the high window she could see the bay, and the light from the window raised swirls of sequiny dust. Rockmother's brace was there, the one for her back. The doctor made her wear it, her back bad, he said, because she was carrying two people in weight. Halfbaby can remember her wearing it like a skeleton on the outside of her body. But Rockmother outgrew it long ago, grew a third person, and Halfbaby can't believe that it ever snapped around her like a slatted coat. Sometimes she crawls into it and lies on her back, imagining her stomach pouching out, her breasts swelling and swelling until she fills the brace like her own rib cage. But Rockmother even then was twice the woman she is.

She sits in the attic now, thinking about chickens in the poppies run red riot around the marsh farm, and she laughs again thinking about how they walk in two directions at once. Did the tail lead the head or the head the tail?

She can smell the varnish cracking on the high chair, feel the decal of the puddle duck curling from the wood. Someday she'd be sitting in the attic and the decal would be gone, finally crackled into paper, into dust. Then it could spangle the window light, settle in the floor crevices.

There's a pile of guano on the floor by the chimney where the bats hang and a neat little pile of delicate bones—mice? voles?—where a barn owl nested once before they puttied glass back into the window frame. She doesn't disturb it. Bones at rest. Pyramids of bones as delicate as ivory straws.

Hornets' nests whisper, their papery cones hanging like bells on the framing ribs. A few water stains near the chimney. Some mortar unchinked and gravelly on the floor.

There's an old immigrant's trunk, its top mounded to shed water, and stuffed with Rockmother's important papers, some old silvery photographs, some papers inked with letters that look like they were written with spider webs. Brown ink on papers as yellow as cream or old tea gloves. Another trunk of linens Rockmother says that she doesn't need but won't throw away. Nobody throws away anything on an island. Somebody took too many pains getting them there in the first place. So the linens wait, staining themselves with patience. Time itself could leave watermarks, Halfbaby knew.

A neat row of shoes, leather curing in the attic heat, wrapped, almost wrapped, in newspaper, the pages uncurling. Time has busy hands. Leather is cured now, but Rockmother's plump feet outgrew the shoes some time ago. Time cures leather and people, Halfbaby knows, hardens them rather than heals them. Cures, cures. The word means twice at once.

Time cures the soaps too, drilled and strung on a rope to dry because it makes the soap last longer, Rockmother says. Enough soap that it will be living here long after she and Rockmother are gone; it gets that hard—like trying to wash with granite.

She rocks the cradle of the back brace with her hand. When it is time for lunch, the window light will cross the first wooden rib of the linen trunk and Halfbaby will bump down the ladder steep steps. And then it's time.

Lunch is cheese sandwiches but first she has to trim the rind like the heel calluses on Rockmother's feet. Beneath the crust, the flesh of the cheddar is still fresh. Rockmother's feet harden under her weight, and Halfbaby has to peel them, too, Rockmother lying face down on the quilt while Halfbaby pares with her sharpest knife. Sometimes Rockmother complains, but Halfbaby knows that she feels it about as much as a mussel shell feels the shucking knife, not at all. Rockmother's flesh is dead and crumbles in her fingers.

Halfbaby watches the chopping blade ease through the firm cheddar. But then she's gone. Watching something else. A boat, prow up, just the bow poking up like a shrine in the phragmites which are rustling, gossipy, over the tip. Clam flats. She can whiff the secret rich muck of it.

"Halfbaby, how you coming with that sandwich?" Rockmother is trying to call her back to herself. The grandmother rocker creaks; it's called a grandmother because it crouches close to the floor. When Rockmother sits in it, Halfbaby can't see the stencil on the black top slat, but she knows that it's there. Its feathery, faded gold, twin daisy eyes like the egg yolks, petals spoking out into a pattern of repeating twinned leaves, which diminish as they repeat until they stop.

Halfbaby's rehearsing the stencil. The slab of cheese stands against the blade.

"I said, Halfbaby, how you coming with that lunch?"

And then the slice of cheese is in her hand, and her hand is laying the cheese out nicely on a bed of white bread, and Rockmother is grunting and creaking again.

"I found his boat," she says.

"How about you find yourself some butter and grill me up that sandwich," Rockmother says.

Rockmother's voice is mad, but she isn't. Not really. More like the warning growl from a fear-biting dog; they don't mean it. Rockmother's voice knows that she is having one of her spells. That's what Rockmother calls them. But they aren't spells. More like side trips. Like time took a side trip and landed at Halfbaby's door, asking for directions. Problem is that Halfbaby never knows where they come from or where they're going. They're just there.

Rockmother tolerates the spells, because people come to Halfbaby for her second sight. That's what they call it, second sight, though Halfbaby isn't sure if she is seeing first or second, forwards or backwards. She just sees. And people pay her for seeing.

After lunch people come to the parlor and want Halfbaby to see. Sometimes she sees; sometimes she doesn't. But Rockmother makes them pay her whichever way. Butter money.

There's an expression makes Halfbaby laugh—when the minister's wife said, "Why I have half a mind to tell her what I think." Halfbaby knew that wasn't what she meant. She laughed because she knew all about half a mind. She lives in the half mind, half here, half somewhere else, another place or time. Above-stairs, below-stairs. Attic and parlor. Here and there. But she doesn't know if, like the yolks, they split or join. But she thinks that it is why she's Halfbaby. Either that she is something extra or she is something missing. Phantom pain, the way she thinks that an amputated leg must feel, or the amputee. But it isn't pain. It can't be pain because it makes her laugh. She is laughing now as she butters the bread, laughing at the minister's wife who doesn't know that she is being funny when she speaks with half her mind.

And Rockmother says, "There's places for people who laugh at nothing." And her voice still burrs like a fear-biter's. But she doesn't mean it. She likes the butter money. And Halfbaby slaps the bread onto the hot skillet and it sizzles, and Rockmother rocks, and the afternoon pours honey thick into the room.

Later Cap Dobbins will knock on the door and Halfbaby will help him find his boat.

Halfbaby sits on the cracked leather of the mahogany chair in the parlor, waiting for Cap. Rockmother is letting herself smother the red settee, her laps spilling out to the sides. Halfbaby is holding herself very still like a cup of tea on a tray. She is waiting to see.

"You having a spell?" Rockmother asks.

But it never happens like that. She doesn't have spells; more like the spells have her. It's like opening a door in your own house and finding a corridor there that you didn't know was there. Like you scale the ladder steps and open the attic door only it's the cellar, and not your cellar, but somebody's because you can smell the use—the sweet rot of forgotten onions, coal dust, rust on the lids of the canning jars. Somebody's been here. Somebody besides you. Somebody is beside you although you are there, too. Like a hand slipped into someone else's glove, a second skin seamed taut over your own.

Halfbaby has a trick to ready herself. She tries to remember backward. Sometimes it helps when her mother rocks, the grunt, and creak, and rock of wood on wood, but there's no rocker in the parlor, so Halfbaby has to play her trick on herself. She tries to remember backward, all the way back to the midwife giving Rockmother her name when her name still was Ruth. But she can't get that far. She can only get as far back as when the words stop. Or before they begin. She is staring at the ceiling, only she doesn't know the word. She is just staring. Light plays over the ceiling, and neither light nor ceiling have names. They are just what they are. But the light tumbles, and Halfbaby hears herself laugh. Then a face blocks out the light. The face is very close. Her hands are before the face. The face is Rockmother's only not hard yet, Ruth's. The light seems to be sparking from her hair which is yellow, not white. And the lips, the mouth mean something. But she doesn't have the language for what they mean. Then the face is gone.

Rockmother says, "You there yet?"

But she isn't. You can't force it. It'd be like opening the attic door at night. She never goes into the attic at night. No light. She waits for the light, or the lightness. Her stomach feels hollow. She never eats until after the parlor. Supper, she eats. But not breakfast, not lunch. But she likes to cook for Rockmother. She is laughing now at the cheese rind.

Rockmother says, "Don't go simple on me."

But she's not. She's not simple. She's just waiting for time to stop scratching around, to figure out like a chicken which way it's headed.

When Cap knocks on the door, she feels a little thrill trill up her spine. She always feels like this when Rockmother brings people into the parlor, because she tries to see what they see, what she and Rockmother look like from outside. She tries to see their squat house with the peely paint, and rotted pilasters on the widow's walk all rotten and askew, leaning like rummies against each other in the wind. She tries to see herself with her eyes closed, sitting straight-backed in the chair at the table. The globe of the hurricane lamp unlit. Rockmother humping herself onto the settee. But she cannot see herself from the outside; it all feels inside to Halfbaby.

She opens her eyes, and Cap is there. He wears a buffalo plaid jacket, a matching cap bunched in his hand. He has a lazy smile. She smiles back. He likes her. Halfbaby is pretty, she knows, because the Cole boy told her so when he was building the gates to keep the sisters in the house. Rockmother came and got her and told him to build himself a gate, but Rockmother didn't need to worry. The Cole boy was old even then, before he went to the mainland. Halfbaby didn't care about any old man like Cole boy. But she likes Cap's lazy smile, and his eyes. They have no hurry-up about them.

But Rockmother's all hurry-up. She says, "Sit down and get on with it. We haven't got all day."

But he moves slow into the matching chair at the table like he knows otherwise, like he knows all day is exactly what they've got.

"I've seen your boat," Halfbaby's says. "Least I think it's yours."

"Have you now," he says and slaps his hat on the table, and it seems like too much gesture for Rockmother because Halfbaby hears her flap and re-form under her dress like startled jello.

"I think so."

"Don't that beat all. Where you see it?"

Halfbaby shakes her head, just half a shake. "In the reeds. Clam flats. I can smell some pogies rotting."

"Jeezum," Cap says. "That's not much help. Could be anywhere."

"Could be anywhere but it's not," Rockmother says. "It's not on the ocean."

Cap twists away from Halfbaby and she can feel the cords tighten in his neck. "That's like saying it's not on the moon."

She feels his cords tighten on her neck now. Then she's there and not there. But it's not the boat. Not mud. She sees. Sees some other darkness. But it's muck, too. Smells blood. But not clean like blood—salt and metal—sharp and used up like ammonia, like cellars. She can't breathe. Choking on blood and that smell and the one who lies beside her, choking her, choking with her?

Cap says, "Mud. Mud is everywhere. Reeds everywhere too. How do I know that it's even my boat."

Halfbaby's trying hard to breathe, sees red, tastes red, her mouth gaping. She feels like a fish from the inside. Hooked. Hook with a rusty barb. Mouth full of rust.

"See what you're doing," Rockmother says. "See what you're doing to the girl."

"Girl, shit. She's older than I am."

The room bulges. Halfbaby feels like a jellied eye centering the room which curves away from her everywhere. Rockmother is grunting, but it is taking her a long time to get up. Then she's up and pulling Halfbaby's hands away from her neck where she's clawing herself. Rockmother's trying to unbend her hands, saying "See what you done."

Cap is still smiling lazy at her when she comes back. He's shaking his head. "Quite a show you put on."

Halfbaby feels the sucking squooshy sound that the mud makes when it releases your boot and then she can see the umbrella tree and she knows where she is. "The hook," she says. Her breath comes hard. "Your boat's free. It's down by the hook. The silty side. Blue boat," she says. "Blue boat."

"I'll be damned." Cap is standing. His hat is on his head, one ear flap jutting out. He's unfolding money into Rockmother's hand. Her hand looks yeasty, unbaked next to his. His hand is chap-hard and the nails are rimmed with grease. Dark crescent moons.

Halfbaby thinks that, flap down, he looks like a half-basset, but he is gone before she can say so. Gone hunting, half-hunting like half-bassett. Then Rockmother is stroking her neck and saying, "I thought that you were going to strangle yourself the way you went at your throat."

Halfbaby swallows the half-bassett howl. Halfbaby is tired and hungry. Long trail. Too long. "I went too far," she says. "I went too far back."

And Rockmother is trying to shush her, stroking her hands. Her hands feel wet and sweet on Halfbaby's, the way grape mash feels before it's jelly.

"I'm not sure about the boat," Halfbaby says. "I'm half sure, but I'm not sure."

"It doesn't matter," Rockmother says. "He only gave me three dollars. You get what you pay for."

Then Halfbaby hears Rockmother clattering in the kitchen. Rockmother will fix her supper—maybe beans, she's very handy with beans—and brown bread, always brown bread with beans. A double yolk, lucky dinner. And then one of the sisters will stray by as they sometimes do and that will be today.

Then Halfbaby can dream like she does when she's awake only no one will pay her. And she won't need to worry about whose dreams they are and where they come from because she'll be asleep. Maybe she'll dream the blue boat. Blue boat. Maybe she won't. Wherever the blue boat is, that's where it is.

The sisters do not stray over. There is supper, brown bread, baked beans, grilled ham. Rockmother counts the butter money while Halfbaby washes the dishes, then goes to bed. In bed Halfbaby waits for sleep. She runs her finger down the seam on her side. She cannot see it because she cannot see herself from the outside, but she knows that it is there because she can feel it with her finger, a seam like a seam in a glove running up and down. She thinks that it must be how the dreams sneak in while she sleeps. The way a tide noses a blue boat out or in. The way a stain weaves into linen, ink into paper. A seam in time. Yolks in a bowl staring cross-eyed at the flour sifting down.

It snows. Halfbaby wakes up to snow. That cannot be right. There are still flowers snaggling the gardens at the marsh farm, but there they are, heads poking up through the snow. So it snows.

Rockmother is already downstairs. She isn't waiting for Halfbaby. Halfbaby smells bacon.

"It snowed," Rockmother says when she enters. "Means hard winter. I'm going on the ferry to get a few things. Be gone all day. You stay inside till I get back."

Halfbaby nods. She wants to be cooking the bacon instead of Rockmother. She doesn't want to go outside. Rockmother's boots flap around her ankles where she can't close the zippers. An egg plops onto the skillet beside the bacon, shrivels. A single yolk.

"No luck" she says.

But Rockmother hears 'no lock'. "No lock," she says, "but you don't have to let anyone in. No one will be out in the snow anyway."

But Halfbaby knows that it isn't true because Rockmother is going out. Then she does.

Halfbaby watches her tracks in the snow filling up till she can no longer see tracks. But then the sun cracks out. Cracks like an egg. Rainbows sparkle everywhere on the snow. She watches. Then no rainbows, no snow, just the tracks, little mounds of footed snow, mashed, leading away from the house. The world is wet and shiny.

Halfbaby watches the world from the attic window. Snow, then puddles. Some of the flowers shake themselves in the marsh farm gardens, unbending, standing up straight again. Slowly. The air is damp, sunny, and cool. It is fall, but it smells like spring. One of the sisters tilts outside, her black triangle of a coat sharp against the white clapboard of the farm. First, she looks like a wet leaf on a stick, then closer, larger, like a scarecrow but with a hat like a crow, trim and black, feathered. Then close up, she is Lily. Then gone. Halfbaby cannot see her, but she hears a knock on the door. When she opens the door, Lily is in the parlor.

Lily has a look like Halfbaby knows from the inside, like she's happy to be there but she isn't certain where she is. She has a can in her hands in her coated lap. The sisters always bring gifts when they call, but they forget that they have them.

"Now what is this," Lily says. She stares at the can of evaporated milk in her hands. "Did you give me this?" she asks.

"No," Halfbaby says, "you brought it."

"Then," Lily says and she sets the can on the table.

Halfbaby smiles and says, "Thank you."

Halfbaby does not know how much time elapses before Lily starts visiting. When she does, it's like she's wound like a clock, a story that must tick out. She is talking about Rose and the Cole boy. "So many babies then. That spring. Strange weather, like the weather itself gone shack-wacky, wanted to break out—hail and sun. Omens like Ruth's baby, born about the same time as Rose's. Ruth's baby, the two-sided one, she was going to cut it down to size herself, tried to. Blood everywhere. But it wasn't murder. No sin. She was trying to clean it up."

Lily is rocking although she isn't in a rocking chair. Memory swings her pendulum. "Cold, though, to cut your own child. The midwife said she was like a rock."

Rock. Halfbaby is listening and not listening, the way snow is there and melting at the same time. She shivers. She is cold or frightened.

"But the mainland doctor, he cleaned it up. Throwed half the baby away. The other half growed up fine. They say so. Who knows anything at all. I saw a two-headed cow once until one of the cows moved. I know a boy raised, whose sister was actually his mother and made him uncle to himself. Who knows the truth?" She nods; her pale blue eyes clot with pearls.

Halfbaby is there and not there. She wonders if Lily can see through the pearls. She is very still: Rockbaby now. But Halfbaby knows the truth. She wants to ask about names, but she knows that you don't name what you throw away, just what you keep: Halfbaby. But no matter how she cut it, they were two with the same name: Halfbaby. Halfbabies.

Lily is staring at the can of evaporated milk, her eyes wide, the pupils are round and large like Black-eyed Susans; the black-blues rolling with the pearls. Her breath is coming in shallow pants. Her eyes are spooked like a horse's, roll white and wary like she's waiting for that can of condensed milk to do something any second, unlatch the gates and let time come stampeding in or out. She is lost again and Halfbaby will have to help her get her bearings, map out the walk home to the farm next door.

Halfbaby says her name several times: Lily, Lily, Lily. Lily stares at Halfbaby like she stared at the can; she doesn't know how they got there. She doesn't know what they will do next.

But Halfbaby knows: the can will be a can. Halfbaby will be Halfbaby. Halfbaby knows: WHERE is the place that I am standing in. WHERE is always the place. Not a question.

When Lily is gone, Halfbaby is happy because she can rock in the rocker and know what she knows. Not the Cole boy way of knowing, the other way of knowing—knowing what you already know—if you can just get still enough to listen. Rocking and drifting in a bright blue boat.

Rockmother, savage with pain. Savage with killing and birthing. Which half, mother, do you keep as you make your correction? Rock. Mother. Which half do you love, Halfbaby? Which half hate? Until the doctor crosses from the mainland to fix it, but too late to heal. He saves half.

Halfbaby divides time. Not like numbers. Time divides. Time divides itself. It's not counting. But she knows what counts. *Count*'s another word that means twice at once.

She doesn't feel that something is missing; more that she is what is missed, that out there her half-sister-self looks for her. Halfbaby understands now that what she sees is what her sister-self sees for her while she is looking, looking for her—restless in some place that she cannot imagine, mainland, some vast place, foggy with souls impatient for bodies. Mainland. There.

Here is island and rock and Halfbaby waiting to be found by her self-sister who isn't dead because she was only half always and half rocks here. A thought waiting to occur. A blue boat in the reeds. A boot mucked deep in the mud.

What does it mean to have half your sight adrift? But Halfbaby somehow has bone-knowledge, blood-sureness that we all have shadow selves, slipping moorings. She just isn't sure, isn't absolutely sure which half she is. The half who's gone or half who's here. Everywhere we grope in attics for our absences. Time slides. Mice fill corners with chewed wedding dresses. Chimney sparrows nest in eaves of time, nests woven from other nests, something old, something new. And Halfbaby knows, too, why her world is man-less. She was born married. Like Rockmother read in her book of Ruth:

Intreat me not to leave thee: for whither thou goest, I will go: and where thou lodgest, I will lodge. Where thou diest, will I die, and there will I be buried.

Ruth a twice word, too—a name and a name for sorrow and mourning and pity. Ruth. Ruthless. Rockmother.

And Halfbaby knows that she is already dead and already alive. Buried aboveground with one eye cocked here, one there, time collapsing like a telescope between them. Halfbaby knows what she has always half-known, that half of her is out there waiting in a blue boat on the sea, the limbo sea of the unborn for Halfbaby to join her. She rocks. She's in no hurry. She knows where she is now, time running a seam between her and her. And when Rockmother comes home with her packages and parcels, tinned goods and flour bags, and dried fruit, she will find Halfbaby rocking backward before Rockmother became rock, before the midwife named her; before the doctor slit Wholebaby's world; before blood; before time, rocking—Halfbaby but holy, her cock-eyed eyes; and Halfbaby wholly there.

A twin reflection sliding wavery over the water, dappling time. To find. To be found.

Blue boat. Blue boat.

The Fox

THE MAN AND WOMAN stand barefooted among the debris washed ashore. They shout at each over the swashy surf. Overnight, tropical storm Diana whirled in and laundered the sky to a cool beach-glass blue. The surf strains; the winds whip with Diana's residual agitation. The man is shouting, "Horseshoe crab," and pointing.

"Horseshoe crab," she repeats, but she's distracted by a whelk half buried in the sand. She digs it out with her toes.

They are trying to fall in love. But she finds it gets more difficult as one gets older. Experience makes optimism harder; time makes it more necessary. She returns to him and they hold hands, grinning, their hair salt-stiffened, their skin sand-glittered, trying to be as hopeful and airy as this wind-swept day hung out starchy clean for them. She squeezes his hand once and releases it. She stoops for a wet, black stone which cradles flat in her palm, fitted smooth and hard. Wishing-stones, her late father called them. She skips the rock into the surf and resumes her search for the funky little beach treasures, starfish, whelks, crab pincers with their alluring but sad mortal smell, fishy, like sex just past desire's pitch. She bundles her finds into her discarded over shirt, adds them to the collection of razor clam shells, angel wings. Oh, she wishes she had angel wings, could fly, riding the currents, playful like the gulls. But, at forty, always a past year or two throbs a note dark and deep in the staff reminding her, these remaining years are grace notes.

She fashions a handle out of the sleeves of her faded striped shirt and swings the bundle, tries to look carefree. But he isn't watching her. He's hoarding his own fortune of driftwood, small wedges bored with holes in random runic designs straining to signify like sandpipers' scritchy hieroglyphs on the hard wet band of beach, the I CHING not cast but scattered like pick-up sticks. Everywhere, the mystery of meaning, but no decoder ring. She wishes he would look up at her, but his head remains lowered. He scoops the pieces of wood into the pouchy pockets of his shorts.

She sashays for her own benefit then, smirking at herself, at the cynicism she can't suppress, feeling as if she's newsprinted on the day: DIVORCED FEMALE 40ish seeks beachcomber for laughter, sun, surf and possible commitment. And she falters, wondering why she has come out here to Assateague with him. Why bother at all? Why risk it? Wondering if she really has the energy to begin again.

Then he looks up at her, his face, a wonder, sun and wind-buzzed, ruddy. Her hope perks. She remembers his skin, salty to her tongue, the thick mat of his hair tangled like eel grass in her fingers, the bud of his penis in her mouth, his catching breath. But afterwards, her damp thighs drying to him, cementing them together, she felt his sadness notated a beat beneath her happiness. After love-making, she always felt her most fully alive, most purposeful. She transcended, rounded, wombing the world with a sigh. But men dipped into a following sadness. Lying with him, she couldn't bear his quiet, his regret that something, some white liquid fire had been stolen from him, that, rat-like, the darkness nibbled at the edges of this perfectly cut wedge of time. Of course, he had said none of this. What he had said was, "I could really go for a sandwich. You hungry?"

She slings her bundle over her shoulder and splashes out into the water. It ruffles around her calves. He sloshes after her, bearing his horseshoe crab shell. The undertow, like desire, like Diana's greed, sucks the sand from beneath her soles, and she shifts to keep her stance. He reaches her and extends the carapace like a bowl. She stares into it. Fill me, fill me, the shell urges, but she cannot hear it for the waves, for the wind which is knotting cat's paws in her hair. She rattles through the jumble of shells and finds the whelk, raises it to her lips and blows the low whistle out of the whorls. He touches her cheek lightly, his fingertips daubing her skin with the wet-dry saltwater.

"Look," he says, and he flips the shell over and rubs the encrusted spiny back with his fingertip, the carapace studded with cabochons of abalone, barnacles. "Some of them live to be one hundred and fifty years old."

"Not this one," she says.

"Who's to say?" He shrugs. He tests his finger against the spindle of the telson. "Would you like it?" he asks.

"No thanks." She suppresses a shudder at the horny, over-inhabited look of the shell. It's dead history, a souvenir helmet from a short-lived war. She presses the whelk shell hard into the hardness of his chest and kisses him, sudden and wet, and hopes as she pulls away from him he will be smiling. He is, but his brow creases, too.

"Come on," he says. "Let's walk." And he tugs her, leading her from the roiling breaking water.

They stroll and talk desultorily. She tells him about the train ride down from Newark, about the man who came to their car pleading for money. "Can you help me, please? I've got $12. I just need another $7.80 to get home. Please. Anyone?"—how most people, she included, ignored him. Then a hand fluttering a dollar bill above a headrest down the aisle shamed her. She fished a bill from her wallet, but the panhandler had worked his way to the rear of the car. He didn't return and take her dollar. She'd felt cheated.

"Probably he works the station to score drugs," the man says.

"Perhaps," she says. "But then all the more reason for him to get home."

He mocks her innocence. "Don't you get it? He wasn't going home." He snickers, but he squeezes her hand, clearly touched. "How have you survived to middle age as a naif?" he asks her.

"By being cynical," she says and pokes him in his love-handled side. At forty, she knows the rhythm of courtship, a scansion of gesture, repartee. Beauty sags downward from the eye of the beholder to the mouth of the bespeaker. "Besides," she adds, "for whatever reason, he needed the dollar more than I did."

But she's lost his attention again. "Shipwreck," he says, pointing down the beach to a thick black line scrawled across the white sand. As they approach the wreck, its mossy, waterlogged hulk, they see the near side's flat like a pier but the far side is ribbed like a boat. They walk around it, curious, rubbing rust stains with their fingers, palming the salt-bit, creosoted timbers, the corroded iron rings, the chipped cleats.

"A pier," she supposes.

"But the curve," he says.

"A barge?" she asks.

"A barge," he repeats, this possibility settling in him. Then something distracts him again. She never seems to hold his interest long enough.

"Come," he says, pulling on her hand. "I saw something. Maybe it's one of the wild horses. But it looked smaller. A raccoon? There," he says pointing at the crest of a dune. "There."

She stares toward the slatted sand fence, sees only the fence and the banking sand. But she follows his insistence across the beach. As they leave the peopled area for the fenced-back area, she notices fewer shells, ghost crabs barely visible, protectively colored, betraying themselves only by their scuttle among the rubbish beyond the tide's reach: plastic milk jugs, forks, squishes of plastic wrap. The waste, the audacity of the waste, she thinks, angry, until she breasts the dune and sees what he's seen—a fox lapping at a hollowed pool concealed from the beach. Head bent, tongue flicking.

They stand very still, gazing.

"He's drinking long," the man says.

"It mustn't be brackish. Rain water from Diana?" she says.

"Yes. I guess that's it." He smiles at her. "Let's get closer."

"Move slowly," she says. "We don't want to startle him." As they descend the dune, their heels catch and skid through the sand. But the fox doesn't shy; he keeps drinking. She thinks at any minute he will spook, scent them, hear them with his long rabbity ears and hightail over the dunes. But he only drinks. Lap, lap, lap—they approach close enough to hear him, no, her, she corrects herself. Once, the fox's head yaws, just acknowledging them; then she resumes lapping, tail high, not curled, ears taut and alert but not bent in mistrust. They come within three feet of the fence and stop. The fox keeps drinking.

"We're downwind," she whispers. "She can't smell us but she should hear us. Deaf?" But, no, the fox jerks her head up as the woman whispers.

The man clutches her hand and presses it tightly against his hip. "Maybe she's so used to people, she's tame."

The comment reminds her of a story. "Once with my first husband, Clinton, I saw a yearling deer like that. Our foundling. We were driving up my parents' dirt road in Vermont when we spotted the deer. We parked. The deer stared. We opened our doors. The deer stayed. We neared her, close enough to stroke her muzzle. She never shied. It made us sad. We knew, untutored in people as she was, she'd be bagged in the next deer season. We had to shoo her off, flailing our arms, hollering."

"Hush," he says, and she realizes he hasn't been listening to one of her favorite stories, that he's been attending only to the fox. So she, too, attends to the fox who, head lowered, is trotting, sniffing along the urine-spritzed boundaries of her territory. She's contouring the fence perfectly, geometrically.

How to Stop Loving Someone

As the fox trots by, but two feet before them, the woman sees the fox's right eye, blinkered shut with pus. Her left eye, true, roves over their bare feet. Then the fox pivots, militarily precise, through a hole snapped into the slats in the fence segment before them. Neither harried nor tentative, she paws a nest in the southern, sunlit sand and curls into it.

The fox admits their presence, craning her neck, fixing them with her good eye before she flips onto her back and squiggles, a moment of pure animal happiness the woman envies. Then the fox rolls back onto her stomach and snouts in the sand. The woman reflects on the adjectives usually applied to foxes: sly, shrewd, cunning. All imply duplicity. But this fox appears sincere and composed.

"Come," the man says. "I think we can get closer."

She hesitates behind him as he approaches the fence. "We don't want to rush it. We don't want her to run off, spoil it. . . ."

But he steps up to the corner of the fence and balances his forearms on the red slats.

She expects the fence, a flimsy roll of laths wired together, to bend under the weight. She can't imagine that its insubstantial strips actually manage to tame the storm-hurled sands, but apparently they do or the rangers wouldn't bother with them.

He turns to her. "Come," he says again. "Please."

The fox rises, shakes herself before nesting again, her head on her paws facing them, neither afraid nor overly curious, merely aware.

Carefully, the woman advances, rests her arm on the fence beside his, slides her hand into his. She realizes she's grinning, that her mouth aches from grinning. She stares into the fox's good eye.

"How old is she, do you think?" he asks.

The woman considers. Up close, the coat is ragged, ratty not glossy as she'd expected. "She's small," the woman says. "But females often are. She might be young, an abandoned pup." But she speculates without conviction. The fox could be any age. As she pants, her rib cage protrudes, grooving her sides as if death were pressing its skeletal way out of her body. But the fox's face points young and sharp, and the woman withdraws into a moment of conscious awe at getting this close to an animal usually so stealthy, so secretive, one who skirts the furtive darkness.

His hand pulls hers again, teasing, urging her forward. "Let's go behind the fence." He tugs, presses, always ulterior.

"No," she says, fearful that surely now the fox will bolt. But he leads her, and they inch their way to the end of the sand fence, corner it. Inside with the fox, he says, "Sit. Sit slowly." And she eases herself cross-legged to the ground, nestling her bundle in her lap. The fox lifts her head.

The woman can see the fox's haunches tense. The high thighs, muscled for speed, twitch, but the fox only snuffles, appraising the danger.

"I can't believe this," the man says, sitting next to her. "Do you think she's sick? She drank for such a long time, and her eye—"

"Maybe that's it," the woman interrupts. "She's very thin." She considers, rabies? But the fox lies contentedly near the water. She shakes her head, wonders at the three of them: a woman, a man, a fox. She reaches to take his hand, but it shuns her. He's fussing with his pockets.

"Shit. I wish I'd brought the camera," he says.

"Isn't this enough?" she asks.

And he looks at her quizzically, but he doesn't answer.

His restless hands disturb the fox who rises slowly but imperturbably and trots to the hole in the fence, ducks through and lies down on just the other side of it. The woman can't help herself; she blurts a laugh. Inquisitive, the man looks up at her, but she can't bring herself to tell him what she's thinking: that the fox knows just how much distance to maintain between itself and the other, just how much intimacy it can bear, permit, just how much proximity to allow. The fox is wiser than they. Wild hearts keep a fence between.

The man, still disappointed with the missed opportunity, the camera snugged under the car seat, sighs. She smiles at him and flattens her palms on his sun-warmed thighs.

Eventually, lazily, the fox rouses, pads back to the pool, drinks long, then sprints over the dune. The man hugs her then, takes her by surprise. And something twinkles, the silica dusting his cheek, an inkling of the possible life, the alternate one, the one that might have been.

A sharp face. Then a glimpsed tail.

If It's Bad It Happens to Me

HERE'S ANOTHER THING nobody tells you; cowboys can smell women. Austry Ann is in front of me, (her name is Australia, Australia Ann. I don't know what her parents were thinking; I guess that they were feeling colonial). She is entering the smoky beery darkness of the Continental Club on Soco, and, without even turning around, the cowboy in the lizard print hat has a bead on her. It's in the tightening of his shoulders, the twist to his hips. He is on her like chocolate on coconut, like cupids on valentines, like salsa on a fajita. He turns his head then, cool and slow. Then he gasps, he really does, as if he's just been sucker-punched in the gut by some Friday night roustabout. And who can blame him? Hell, even I know that Austry Ann makes seeing men blind, and talking men dumb. She's got a shelf that you can display calacas on. Hips that were invented to be riveted to Levi's. Tonight she's wearing a plum top so tight that it could be inside her and it comes to a little triangle hem in front so that you can catch a glimpse of her skin either side. She's bopping to the pumping fusion already that some local girl is blasting out of her axe. Austry

How to Stop Loving Someone

Ann's hair is flipping around, her long tangled, shock-waves of red hair, and the cowboy is asking her to dance. It isn't always easy being her friend.

The cowboy is two-stepping her onto the sweaty dance floor. It's crowded. Don't get me wrong. I love Austry Ann. How not to? But around Austry Ann you get used to being a gaping ape of a sidekick. You learn how to smile like you enjoy standing alone, enjoy getting pushed around in a jammed bar, enjoy watching your beautiful girlfriend dance. It takes practice. Patience too. Especially tonight because I am in stiletto heels. They are not dancing shoes. Hell, they are not even walking shoes. They are I-got-glam-legs-but-am-too-stupid-to-walk shoes. Austry Ann has the beauty and the dazzle. But I got height. It gives me a vantage point.

And here's the point. It's late. It's around 1:30 when the cowboy starts pitching into the drum set. Jimmy Buffet can sing until every tourist mourns his Mexican cutie through the punt of a Jose Cuervo bottle; I am here to tell you that Margaritaville is Austin, Texas. This time the cowboy doesn't extract himself from the cymbals, so Austry Ann tells me that we are calling it a night. It was a night four hours ago. It was a night all night long, but I keep that to myself. As she leaves the Continental Club, Austry Ann is breaking hearts. One soused cowboy grabs me by the arm and says, "Hey, ladies, it ain't even closing time."

"We're just drunks going home," I say. And we are.

I don't have a job yet, so in the morning we decide to play. Austry Ann works nights at a gallery, Blue Cactus. They import retablos and Katrinas from desperate Mexicans, jack up the prices, and sell them to the turquoise-studded tourists. I moved in with Austry Ann two weeks ago, but I am not sure that it's going to work. For one thing, Austry Ann has a temper. I mean temper. When she goes off, it is so sublime that you might believe that she is holy. She's a saint of temper, the Mother Teresa of temper.. And she does go off. And you never know when. When there's no milk for the coffee or the lizard-figured shower curtain isn't pulled all the way across.

Once in New York City I saw a burned car. The dashboard was puffed up into something that looked like burned marshmallows. That's how Austry Ann's heat makes me feel. Toasted. Charred. It makes me quiet.

Then she will do something so beautiful or so funny that you know it's safe to venture out again. Last week when I told her that I liked her ankle bracelet, she just popped it off and popped it on me. And when we were out last Thursday she sauntered up to some stranger on the street with nostalgic hair. Nineteen-forties sausages of hair, lacquered into place with gravity defying techno-hairspray. Austry Ann said, "I just love your retro look."

The woman stared and spluttered. She'd been keeping that coif in her closet and trotting it out every day since Roosevelt went on the radio. We laughed until there was nothing funny left in the universe. Not to be mean. It was just an accident.

"Austry Ann," I said, "you are more fun than things that are not fun."

Okay, and for another thing . . . I mean besides the temper.

But that's enough right there: the temper. Maybe this living arrangement won't work.

This morning Austry Ann screams, "Toast. The last piece of toast."

I know that she means bread. I wait it out.

"The last fucking piece of toast. What am I? The last fucking runt piglet to the tit?"

She goes on for a while. After Austry Ann's wildfire about my eating the last slice of cinnamon bread burns out, we're headed to the costume store on Soco. I don't know why. For laughs. Because we haven't been there yet. It has a neon parrot sign and Elvis and Marilyn Monroe in the window which feels about right. Down here cars and buildings last forever. You keep feeling as if the globe were whirling backward. And when you read the news, you wish it were.

Austry Ann says that she wants to go canoeing after that which is okay with me. Sounds soothing. Water is soothing.

On the plane to Austin I looked down and thought that I saw water, Jimmy Buffet water, with giant sea turtles scudding through. Then I realized that it was all sky, sky in every direction, and the turtles were the tops of clouds making their leisurely way. They didn't even need flippers. There were—it took me a while to identify them—pellets of ice falling through the sky. White landing on blue, like a swan startling in Boston Gardens, like the purity of deep ice, and I thought it was an omen, that Austin would be all right. In the sky, you forget about news, about a Texan invading Iraq which is far away, because in the sky everything is far away, even you, and nobody knows where you are, because you didn't tell anyone, not even your old boyfriend. You are leaving him just like Austry Ann is leaving her husband. Finally. She and her husband haven't lived together since you met her. In New York. On the street. Near the burned out car. Right after 9/11 when people were going to witness, to mourn. But that wasn't why Austry Ann was there; she was there to serve papers on her husband. But that was where we met. On the street. She came right up to me. Austry Ann is outgoing.

After canoeing, she needs to go to the notary public, something about her divorce papers. She pronounces it, "Noter republic." It irritates me less than you might imagine. It's cute like the scrunchi with the poodles on it that she uses to pull back her hair.

But me? No noters, no public. I just upped and left my boyfriend. What can I say? It was the sort of affair that could have only begun on a floor. And it had. He was crashing on my girlfriend's floor in Boston, recovering. Heroin, I think, then alcohol. Americans are recovering from everything, themselves. I was staying with my girlfriend because I didn't know where to move to next. After Boston. Not Boston actually. Allston. But the Boston area. It seemed like a good time to leave. Boston is next, I think, the next target. Prudential Building I bet.

My boyfriend and I used to go to Jack's Joke Store in Boston. It wasn't funny. A novelty act, a novelty store. I opened a box. It said, "What every girl wants." Inside, a lei. A cheap one, no flowers, the kind that gassed people wear at suburban barbecues in July. I didn't get it until

Jack looked embarrassed. At least I think that it was Jack, think he looked embarrassed.. It wasn't funny. Little is. My boyfriend laughed himself senseless. No observable difference there. So I left.

Now I am here. And we, Austry Ann and I, are going to the costume shop. Then canoeing. Then the noter republic.

The costume shop careens with color like Peewee's Playhouse, all chairy and cheery, all color and queasy like Memphis with a hangover, like Elvis on drugs. I nod at the punctiliously pierced child with the punk tufts, magenta, behind the counter. "Nice window," I say. "Marilyn, Elvis."

"Yeah, Elvis. Iraq and roll." He leers, and he and his vacuous vampire co-worker skirl into whip-it giggles.

What is wrong with these people? Then I pause because they are my people, too.

It's strange in here. Bright and cheerful, almost manic. And dirty. Say you set PeeWee Herman, masturbatory interior decorator, loose in your house. The furnishings are cartoonish, but you wouldn't sit anywhere. The source of *that* stain? It may not be a comical spot. Not good clean fun. It may not be lemonade. Maybe marital aid.

Austry Ann is ahead of me and staring at rows of masks. Rows and rows of heads—Mickey Mouse, Ronald Reagan, Jason, George Bush, Goofy, George Bush Redux—stacks and stacks of historical heads like Mme. Guillotine runs the shop. The SpongeBobs and ET's, Margaret Thatchers and Darth Vaders.

Vampire Girl swishes her fishnetted legs and leans her Goth coif toward Pin Cushion face, and they giggle and gossipily hiss. Then Pinhead looks at us as if we're homeless people who have blundered into Prada or something and asks with a flip of the wrist that a sitcom fag wouldn't risk, "Do you fillies want help?" But he's turned back to his vamping cohort before we can answer.

We wander into the catacombs of parti-colored costumeland. Entire racks of leather lingerie and *Gone with the Wind* bustled gowns, parasols. I try to imagine them together, Melanie stripping off her demure gown to her patent leather Merry Widow and smacking Ashley with a riding crop. It's troubling how easy it is to imagine that. Gone with the whinny.

Austry Ann bumps my hip with hers. "This place scares me a little. How do you think they stay in business?"

I wonder the same. Halloween, sure. Mardi Gras. The occasional costume ball. But it would take a lot of gay clubs to support a place like this. And I doubt that there are a lot of gay clubs in Texas. There was only one cowboy in the Village People.

I follow Austry Ann past the feather boas and the dressing cubicles which are action-painted in primary colors, past the funhouse mirrors, and the screaming meemie murals until we reach the shoe racks, and I stop like a spring-less jack-in-the-box. There they are. Ruby slippers. And I really am ready to go home already, but I no longer know where home is—not Boston. Not here.

It becomes fun for a while, playing dress-ups in the back alleys of the store. I click my ruby-dusted heels, and Austry Ann starts camping it up like Aunt Bea, right down to the Mayberry dither. It's a little karaoke-hokey but fun until I hear something that doesn't sound fun. That sounds like wailing, and it is.

I look at Austry Ann and the bib of her Aunt Bea dress is wicking out with tears. Her Bea bun of domesticated hair is bobbing as she sobs. I mean sobs. Weeps. The sort of weeping that makes you think of willows and engravings of them, curving over a headstone with a short poem below, mourning for a child. Usually the graveyard has a stream.

Austry Ann is streaming. Her face is a mask of itself, her body lost in the absurd Bea dress with her blue jeans underneath. And I am uncertain what to do, so I hug her. Her Bea pop-it pearls press like a chain into my chest. What links us.

"What is it, Austry Ann? Whatever is wrong?"

She can't get the words out, and she's soaking my shirt. I just keep patting her Mayberry bun and asking her what's wrong.

Finally she gets out, "Everything. Everything is wrong. If it's bad, it happens to me."

Round and round the Mayberry bush, I keep mumbling, consoling until Austry Ann tugs the Bea dress, using the bib to wipe her nose, her eyes.

When we leave, the slacker clerks glance up at us for an instant as if we might be borderline interesting. Austry Ann is a mess. Mascara like an oil spill. Face jalapeno red. Hair an uncoiling Monty Python of a bun. She sticks her tongue out at the clerks who resume gossiping. We're across the border, no longer interesting.

It's the SxSW festival in Austin, and the streets are lousy

with musicians and roadies and film people and newspeople and tourists.

There's some retro punk scene exploding here, so carpenters are pounding away, constructing stages behind the restaurants high enough to vault the moshers.

Retro punk. Like the Goth Punk costumers, deliberate stereotype retro-actors. Retro punk. Stupid. America's been a punk since Elvis and Marilyn went under glass. And I miss them. Their glamour. The sureness in life that all you needed was a full tank of gas, tunes on the dial, an accommodating backseat, and long highways everywhere leading to neon lit promises.

Austry Ann and I are canoeing, and I'm glad. Water is nature's valium; Austry Ann's calmed down. She's paddling happily and chatting as we slip past trees, green and fungal in the water, turtles on top like conchos on a belt.

Austry Ann is trying to talk me into going to some opening at the Gallery Lombardi, The Rawk Show, art by all girl punk rockers. It sounds either too specialized or too complicated, I don't know which. But I don't want to spoil the canoe bliss with a fire-breathing scene or a sob-a-thon, so I say, "Why don't we talk about it after we finish up at the notary public?"

I like it here on the river. Time slips by with the ducks and geese. Fish jump. Families laugh. Couples argue. The paddles make a shush shush sound. No motor boats. Beyond, the city looms. High-rises, skyscrapers. Skyscapes have changed forever. I used to think of them as aspiration, ambition, or towers of greed. Now I think of them as targets. It feels odd to be paddling in the shadow of the city. This pace and that pace side by side.

Austry Ann is talking about everything bad that happens to her, and it's easier to listen with the fluid sounds of the river, Austry Ann's voice and the river's deliquescing.

She doesn't like her job. She wants a shot at a film career. And her husband was a creep. And other people just don't know how hard. Splish. Slup. Ripple. Shlup. Burble.

It's okay here on the river. Austry Ann's hair is a fiery corona in the sun. She could be the goddess of Austin. Or Huck Finn's female double. I know who that makes me.

The stop at the notary public doesn't go well. Austry Ann goes in, then comes right back out, sticks her head in my side of the jeep.

"Something about this doesn't feel right," she says.

"What?"

"Something. Would you come in with me?"

"Jeez, Austry Ann, they stamp your paper. You sign your name." But I go in anyway.

It's a little clapboard shotgun with a big vanity sign of the notary public out front, her photo and signature, like she thinks that she's famous or should be. Who puts her name on her own billboard?

I go in, and right away I know that Austry Ann is right. The scene is askew like the floors in that costume shop. No desk, just this fuzzy pit furniture. The whole room is a couch upholstered in some animal print. Cheetah? Leopard? Like a weird modular interplanetary cubic cat-thing has landed and is taking up residence wall to wall. The woman on the couch looks up at me. I recognize her from her billboard. But her face glazes, like a doughnut. She's got that keen-blurry look of a weed-eater. Stoned. She's wearing pinto printed jeans and a midriff ripped Kiss T-shirt.

Austry Ann picks up a clipboard. Clipboard?

Then I see him. He's sprawling on another pit hassock, grinning. Everything about him tweaks me: trouble. He's got a face like a snapped off hood ornament, shiny, petty criminal, misplaced, smile like a game show host. Red mesh T-shirt. Jeans that must require an inhaler for an accessory. When I read him, I get the cue: BAD ACTOR.

Austry Ann is puzzling over the clipboard, and the pothead is leaning forward now and massaging her shoulder.

Clipboard?

Austry Ann says, "I really don't see why I have to answer all these questions. It's just a financial disclosure. I just need it stamped." But she keeps scribbling.

I am still standing. "Let me see that."

Austry Ann hands it to me.

I read out loud, "How often a week do you and your partner have sex? Do you enjoy oral sex? Do you and your partner incorporate play?" I think I know how the costume shop stays in business.

"Austry Ann, stand up," I say, and she does. The weed woman's hand falls away, lands thunkily like it doesn't know it has dropped.

"Give me your papers," I tell Austry Ann, and she does. I give them to the notary and say, "Stamp these now, and sign it."

I tell Austry Ann to go get in the jeep.

The notary has disappeared through a beaded door, the beads still clacking when she returns. As she rubs her exposed stomach, her puffy bellybutton like a wheel beneath Gene Simmons' jagged face, she tells me her fee for notarizing.

"You must be joking," I say. Then I am back at the jeep with Austry Ann who is crying again.

She says, "See, see. If it's bad, it happens to me. What *was* that?" She leans her head against the steering wheel.

"Who knows. I mean she *is* a notary public, but, Jesus, Austry Ann you don't have to answer personal questions about your sex life to get a financial statement notarized. Maybe they front a singles club or a swingles club. Maybe they are a two person tingles tag team club. Who knows? You walk in, you're beautiful. You're bait. but when it feels creepy, it probably is. Bolt."

Austry Ann shifts gears. Now she's No Tears Austry Ann. She's thumping the steering wheel and ginning up. "SEE. See. It's not my fault I'm beautiful. What? Do I have a sign on me that says, Fuck with me? Is that all people see? I am pretty, got tits, so you can mess with me any way you like. This isn't normal. We should go in there and fucking trash those people. Like my life isn't bad enough. I got a lousy job. I am in the middle of a divorce. I got kinky noter republics trying to crawl up my ass. See, if it's bad. . . ."

I can't help it. "Austry Ann." I have to say it again because she's a yeller. "AUSTRY Ann. You've got a job. In the middle of a recession. You're beautiful. You split up with your husband because you were fucking around. You have a place to live, food. You whine more than anyone I know. We are on the verge of a war. We have an idiot in the White House who wants to maraud into an impoverished country, rip the globe to pieces, expose Americans to retaliatory terrorist attacks. The decision comes Monday, and you are sitting here in a pool of self-pity because two soft core freaks process your papers. What would you ever do with a real problem?"

Austry Ann's poodle scrunchi is popping off her ponytail. "Oh, you don't understand. You don't—"

"But I do understand. That's the whole problem. You are the only person with hardships. Your hardships are luxuries, Austry Ann. Luxuries. And so are your moods."

I turn my head. I can't look at her. She is beautiful even when her mouth is opening and closing, waiting for some words to come, any words, the right words. And they won't.

She surprises me. She says very quietly, "I don't know what's going on in the world."

I am still looking out the window at the dry blasted lawn, the billboard pothead, the clapboard bungalow, the ugliness of it all. "No one does," I lie.

I feel a hand, hers, Austry Ann's on the back of my neck.

I do not turn my head. "I am moving out," I say. That is not a lie.

"You got nowhere to go," Austry Ann says. I hear panic rising in her voice, twitching in the fingers on the back of my neck.

"I know."

It's my last night in Texas. Austry Ann wants to go to San Antonio. To celebrate, she says. She means, commemorate. Maybe she means celebrate. But neither of us is feeling very celebratory. Austry Ann needs to find a new roommate. I told her that maybe she should try that notary public's service. She threw her hairbrush at me, but she was fooling. Me, too.

I have nowhere to go. I took some of my savings from my last job as a temp, what's left over after my plane fare, and bought a 1964 Galaxie convertible. One hundred dollars, cash on the barrelhead. Cars down here are immortal. Not a bad price tag for immortality. The top is ninety-nine percent duct tape, but I'll just pray that the weather holds.

Austry Ann wants to go to Riverwalk. I've never been. And I know that Austry Ann really wants to go because she keeps humming that Patsy Cline tune, *San Antonio Rose*. Bob Wills wrote that song in 1938; he added the lyrics later, 1940, *The New San Antonio Rose.* That's the one that Patsy sings; a lot of people don't know that. Bob Wills and the Texas Playboys.

Austry Ann's singing, "Broken song, empty words I know, Still live in my heart all alone." We're going to San Antone.

We're at Riverwalk listening to an all pipe and whistle band. It echoes on the water and bridges. Tejano music. Haunting, lamenting, beautiful. I am less sure about Riverwalk. I mean, it's pretty, but it looks like someone's idea of Venice, like how Venice would look on that Disney World ride, "It's a small world after all." A literalist named Riverwalk. It is a river (small) and bridges (many). It is shops and restaurants with umbrellas and trees cascading with glittery lights and girls wearing paper flower wreaths. Pretty, but it has a spanking wholesomeness, an artificiality like some project concocted by the Chamber of Commerce. But I am patient. It's Austry Ann's night. Her night out. I am leaving tomorrow and I am clueless where to.

So I walk with Austry Ann and watch the men get lecher's whiplash ogling her. We listen to this band and that, drink Margaritas here and there, eat fajitas, watch the beautiful people watch the tourists watch the beautiful people watch the tourists, all of whom watch Austry Ann.

Tomorrow is Saint Patrick's day. Tomorrow that moron declares whether or not we are going to war. You wouldn't know it by this place. Party on. No Irish about it.

I think that we lost the lesson too fast, the lesson of 9/11. I keep thinking that maybe an object lesson would help. We choose some suburban community like Austin, say, and we just choose a few families and we bomb their houses and kill their children and bomb the schools and hospitals. Just as a lesson in empathy. They'd have to volunteer of course. We'd learn in a hurry. Hell, Americans go haywire when they lose power for an hour. Or cable. We need to remember. Mourning, loss—these are not about infrastructure.

Austry Ann and I are sitting at a café table beside the water at some steak place. Beef is king in Texas. Austry Ann says, "You aren't having much fun on your last night." She's licking salt off the rim of her glass. The flick of her tongue almost levitates the beefy geezer at the next table.

"This is great."

"You need to have more fun," Austry Ann says. "You're too intellectual."

I almost snort frozen lime crystals out my nose.

Austry Ann says, "You know what you need?"

I shake my head. I think about Jack's Joke Store. What every girl needs.

"You need to see the Alamo. That's right. Here you are in Texas, and you haven't seen it. It's famous. I forget why. But you're deep, so you'll appreciate it."

I follow Austry Ann down stairs and up stairs and over bridges and down sidewalks and we turn the corner of some modern office building, and there it is, moonlit, just like in the song. The Mission San Antonio de Valero, as white and shimmery as the moonlight itself. It offers itself to the sky like a prayer, like a votive candle's smoke. How small it looks here, its history dwarfed by the towering office buildings. But it is beautiful.

I grab Austry Ann's hand and tell her so. I am thinking about missions. The first one here, Christian, to convert Native Americans. Later, "the cradle of Texas Liberty," where Davy Crockett died and Jim Bowie. I am thinking how history is a cradle that keeps rocking in one bad actor after another, rocking in, rocking out, rocking on. This luminous building seems too pearly, too pure to be the site of all the blood shed here. I guess that time bleaches all the stains of history. Here every one of the Texan volunteers died, rebelling against the dictator, Santa Ana, who proclaimed victory. But his aide observed, "One more such glorious victory and we are finished."

We do not learn.

"This place is dead," Austry Ann says. "Sunday night. Let's go home." And we do.

Austry Ann is asleep. I pack the Galaxie with the two cases that I brought with me from Boston. I look at the smoggy Austin sky, wish that it were starry, a more propitious omen for departure. I leave Austry Ann a note saying that I'll call (and I will) and I am gone.

It's four in the morning and I am pushing sixty on the Galaxie, pushing fifty myself. Spent the last two decades working as a temp. I suppose that we are all temps in the biggest sense, but here I am now, homeless again and not knowing which way to go. West? Why? *Light out for the Territories?* The rest are all ahead. California or bust? North? South? East? All bust. All busted. The whole country has become a bad joke store.

When I hit Austin's City Limits, I am testifying, I am testifying right out loud to myself in a well-preserved Ford Galaxie. I am the NOTER REPUBLIC, and we are at the limits. Nomadic again, everywhere I go, that's where I am. The continent is shrinking around me like a polyester costume washed one too many times. *One more such glorious victory and we are finished.*

Austin City Limits recently staged a reunion of the Texas Playboys. Bob Wills sold his club in Dallas, the Bob Wills Ranch House, to Jack Ruby. In the fifties. Not many people know that. See, it all relates. History is not stored in small plaqued buildings. History is always now, and these are dangerous times.

I have no idea where I am going, but, if I could, I'd

jam into reverse and drive backward to Elvis, and Marilyn, and Patsy before they became costumes, praying for this country, for some other eventuality, for some other future. Then what? Then what?

I am just driving. I drive. Like cattle driven, I drive.

Got a song on the broken radio: *Where in dreams I live with a memory, Beneath the stars all alone.*

I just keep moving. What else is there to do.

Drive. Driving. Drive.

The Landmark Hotel

ON THE DAY THAT C.C.'s mother did not meet Janis Joplin, "A Boy Named Sue" was a hit record. By Johnny Cash. Ceci hated that song. C.C.'s mother named her C.C. for *C.C. Rider*, the Janis Joplin version, but her friends all thought that her name was Ceci, short for Cecile. Ceci called her mother Dee, short for Deirdre which Dee was fond of telling her was Irish for sorrow. Ceci and Dee. Their boarder, Bobbie, said it was like living in alphabet soup. Or a mediocre report card. Bobbie went to the community college, but it was just the beginning, he said, of a bigger, brighter future in Reality TV. Reality TV is the future, he said.

"Reality TV is an oxymoron," Dee said, crushed her cigarette into the ashtray and peeled a banana at the kitchen table which also served as her desk.

Ceci hated to pick sides.

Here's how Bobbie came to live in their home. It was a nice home, a bungalow from the 30's, maybe a little dark because of the deep front porch and decorated in a style that Ceci thought of as Archeological Bohemian.

Spanish shawls dripped fringe from the walls. Ethnic masks and crude stringed instruments grew beards of dust. Dee's scrapbooks towered on every flat surface. But the bungalow had oak floors and plaster walls like they didn't build them anymore, Dee said. Like the kitchen table which Dee used as her desk, chrome and bright red, a Deco dinosaur. Ceci and Dee loved the house, and Ceci and Dee were broke. They couldn't bear to part with the bungalow, Edifice Complex. The house had an extra bedroom which used to be Dee's office before she took over the kitchen.

Dee never married Ceci's dad. It was the seventies, you know, Dee explained. (Except that it was actually the eighties.) We were all bumbling around the country like Pod People. *Hey man, where you from? Where you going? You smoked some reefer, did some blow, fucked, and hit the road again.*

Sometimes when Dee told the story, Ceci's father's name was Ginger; sometimes it was Cassady. It didn't matter. He was headed, Dee thought, to Mexico and fell off the edge of her map whatever his destination. So Dee raised Ceci. Sort of fly-by-night, sort of catch-as-catch-can, sort of improv theater.

Dee waited tables or flipped short order eggs and burgers and belonged to the local repertory theater group, The Blue Angel Theater Troupe, until the drinking problem got a little out of hand. The theater people, some local gay guys who missed New York and Broadway, some rich civic-minded mavens, were nice about it. *Take some time off. Take care of yourself. Come back when you are better.* Dee wasn't better yet and money was tight, so Dee emptied the office until it was a bedroom again and advertised for a boarder. Hence Bobbie.

And Ceci? Since changing her name in middle school because people kept asking what her initials stood for—Cathy Caroline? Courtney Cherry? Colleen Crystal? Because the moron-a-tons in her class, Robert and that jerkerato Trevor, started the rumor that it stood for the C word, started calling her Cunt-cunt, so she just told everybody that it was Ceci, short for Cecile. She didn't tell them that Cecile meant *blind*, but it did. She'd looked it up. Since then, since Ceci became Ceci, she had helped Dee out. She kicked in her waitressing and baby sitting money. And she'd worked in a video store for a while now. She'd mowed lawns. Not with a riding mower either, but a push mower. 5.5 horsepower. No C.C. Rider.

She'd looked up the lyrics to C.C. Rider too, and she had wondered what C.C. really did stand for. At first, when it was first written, first sung. Did it mean *see* like in the song? *So see C. C. Rider, see what you done done.* The lyrics stuttered. Did it mean *Close call*? *Cavalier convertible*? *Corn cob?*

My home is on the water. I don't like no land at all.

What did that mean? Maybe the C. was *sea*. She was a sea-rider. It didn't matter any longer; Ceci was Ceci in the same way that Bobbie was Bobbie and right now he was see-seeing what he could help-help himself to out of the fridge and Ceci could tell by the way that Dee peered closer at her clippings at her Deco desk that she was reading him right out of print, right out of the kitchen, that Dee hadn't made her mind up about him yet, whether she liked Bobbie or not which was a little complicated because Ceci had fucked him last night for the first time which meant, she supposed, that she wanted to do it again—although Dee didn't know that yet because she hadn't really gotten better like her theater friends had suggested, at least not yet. While Ceci and Bobbie were in a lust clutch, their own little reality show, *Lead Us into Temptation Island*, Dee was in a wine swoon.

Now Bobbie was eating a slab of cold lasagna out of his hand which wasn't really an endearing mannerism, and Ceci wondered why she had tussled with him. She knew from the first that she wasn't attracted to him. He had one of those haircuts that made him look as if his name was Cedric, the deliberate dweeb DO that guys were sporting now. The center twist like a Frosty-cone custard. The one Martin Short's character wore in the SNL reruns, Ed Grimley boinging around the room like a neurotic Chihuahua on an Ecstasy rave trampoline. "That is NOT a good look, I must say."

And the rimless glasses, and the big pants, and the bad tattoo of a spider with its legs in some kind of Celtic knot or maybe it was a web. And now the lasagna in his palm and the slurpy cartoon noises like Mel Blanc eating with a speech impediment. Nope, she wasn't really attracted to him.

"Use a plate," Dee said without turning around.

"In a rush," Bobbie said. "Got a lot of homework."

"You pay room not board," Dee said. exhaling dragon plumes of pale blue smoke.

"I will get him a plate," Ceci said.

Bobbie hoovered the lasagna like a seal swilling a tinker and winked. "Hate to eat and run, doll. The homework calls."

"Translation," Dee said. "There's some meretricious shit on TV that he and a few other million of the walking comatose got to watch."

"Dee," Ceci said. Let's all try to be nice."

"What did nice ever have to do with anything?" Dee asked. She flapped a page of her scrapbook. "The test of a man or woman's breeding is how they behave in a quarrel. George Bernard Shaw."

"Dee," Bobbie said. "What kind of a name is Dee? Sort of a novelty song? Put da lime in da coconut and drink DEE bowl up? It's dee lemon. It's dee lime? Dee feet went over dee fence before dee tail?"

"It's short for Deirdre. It is Irish for sorrow." She patted her henna red curls and struck a pose with her cigarette which once was glamorous; today it was simply cancerous.

"And don't you think it's a little odd, Ceci, for a mother to insist that her daughter call her Dee?" Bobbie headed down the hall. "D for dipsomaniac. D for dysfunctional. D for delirium tremens." His bedroom door slammed. The brassy jingle of a Cruise ship ad blared.

Actually, Ceci did think that it was odd. But it had been odd for a long time which made it seem less odd. Dee for Mom. Not odd at all. Time was like that.

Dee shrugged and glanced at the empty glass by her elbow. Ceci found empty glasses all over the house, full ashtrays and empty glasses. Glasses on the player piano, on the shelves which propped Dee's theater glam shots against dusty books. Dee always pronounced it the-ayter which Bobbie said was an affliction, but Ceci thought that he meant affectation. Empty glasses with amber halos in the punts or rings of carnelian red.

"Would you like some tea?" Ceci asked.

"Did I ever tell you about the time that I met Janis Joplin?" Dee asked.

"You need to get out more," Ceci said.

After Dee went to bed, Ceci stood outside of Bobbie's door, listening to the electric burble of his TV. She wasn't certain about the etiquette involved in screwing your tenant. Should she knock? Should she wait for an invitation. "Bobbie?" No answer. Maybe he couldn't hear her. She knocked. Light caromed into the hall.

"Oh. It's you," Bobbie said. He squinted over his glasses. "I'm doing homework."

Ceci could see the colored lights of the TV play over his rumpled bed.

He slumped against the door jamb. "Yeah, this is great. You ought to see this guy Trump. Looks like he has a drugged ferret on his head. It's aces."

Ceci said, "I didn't know if. . . ."

Bobbie asked, "Have you given any consideration to what you are going to do with your life?"

"No," Ceci said. She hadn't.

"I mean," Bobbie said, "you are nineteen years old and still living at home with a woman who thinks that Bling Bling is a panda and who talks on the phone with Bob the Automated telemarketer. It's sad really."

"She needs me," Ceci said.

"Like Trump needs an apprentice. Look, I got midterms." Bobbie shut the door.

When Ceci got home from clerking at Classic Video, Dee was poring over her scrapbooks, empty glass, full ashtray at her elbow. Uh oh. She smiled a practiced smile that Ceci recognized from the glam shot of Dee in *Blithe Spirit*. "I can resist everything but temptation," Dee said in a dramatic voice which was disconcerting, Britishy but not British, an urchin timbre with class pretensions. "Oscar Wilde. *Lady Windemere's Fan*."

Okeydoke. "Is Bobbie home?" Ceci asked.

Dee grinned. "Guess who got a job?"

"Bobbie got a job?"

Dee propped her chin on her stack of mem books which made it difficult for her to talk. But not impossible. "Moi. It turns out this kid at the community college wants to do an independent project. He wants a drama coach." Dee's jaw worked like a marionette's. "So he called the Blue Angel and guess who they recommended? I guess that they think that I am ready to go back to work."

Ceci wasn't sure of much, but she was quite certain, absolutely completely certain that Dee was not ready to go back to work."

Dee waved a slip of paper. "Here's his name. Jason. Jason somebody." She squinted at the scrap. "Shit, I can't read my own writing."

Ceci took the paper. "I'll take care of it, Mom," she said. "I'll take care of it."

"Dee," Dee said.

Ceci dialed information at the community college and got the listing for Jason Mason. Not much of a stage name. What were his parents thinking? "Yes, Jason. I am calling for Deirdre Moriarty."

"Yes. Who?"

"Is this Jason?"

"Yes."

"I am calling for Deirdre Moriarty. You arranged a class through the Blue Angel Theater Troupe." Ceci stared at the mouthpiece. Odd. "You called requesting her, remember?"

"No."

"This is Jason, right?" Ceci smiled; the response felt eerie, even to her. Is one of us crazy here?

"Jason, yes. But no. Jason. Oh, you must want Jason Mason. He moved out when my girlfriend moved in. Here's the number."

Dee swooped loopily around the room, singing, "Falling in love again, Never wanted to, What am I to do? I can't help it. Love's always been my game." A little distracting. Ceci jotted down the number.

Bobbie peered into the parlor. "Lovely domestic scene."

Ceci said, "Dee's just going through a phase."

"A twenty year phase?" He jammed his hands into his pockets. His boxers puffed over the waist of his oversized pants. Definitely not a good look. Not so much homey as homely. Wasn't it past passé by now?

"She has an addictive personality," Ceci said.

"Not for me."

Ceci twisted away from him and dialed.

Dee struck a posture, an unsteady one. "A community is like a ship; every one ought to be prepared to take the helm." She grinned. "Ibsen. Henrik."

"Not to be confused with the other Ibsen," Bobbie said.

"*From head to toe, I'm made for love*. Lola Lola," Dee said.

"Yeah, Dee. I think therefore I ham."

"I am trying to reach Jason," Ceci said to the phone.

"Speaking."

"I am calling about the theater mentorship."

"What?"

"Is this Jason?"

"Yes."

"I am calling for Deirdre Moriarty about the mentorship you set up through the Blue Angel Theater Troupe."

Dee swiped a shawl off the wall and swept it full of air like a spinnaker. Dust scattered and sifted in little puffs.

"I don't know anything about a mentorship."

"This is Jason, yes?"

"Yes."

"Mentorship?" Bobbie asked. "Dee couldn't mentor her way out of a bottle."

Dee whipped the shawl like a bullfighter. Puff, puff.

"You called about a drama coach."

"Oh, you want the other Jason."

Ceci paused. Dead air. "The other Jason?" she asked. "How many Jasons are there? Do you have a pact to live together or something?"

Ceci pictured a house of Jasons, a tumbling circus of Jasons all clowning around and residing together just for the zany confusion of it all. Oh those madcap Jasons.

"I beg your pardon."

"Did I ever tell you about the time that I met Janis Joplin?" Dee asked.

"I hear that there's a vacancy at the Landmark Hotel," Bobbie said.

"What?" Dee asked.

"Just because I slept with you doesn't mean that I like you," Ceci said. And just then she didn't.

"What?" Jason asked.

"You slept with him?" Dee asked.

"Not you," Ceci said to the phone. "The other Jason. When will he be in? He needs to schedule some appointments with Ms. Moriarty." This was getting complicated.

"Who exactly is this?" Jason asked. "Are you a friend of Jason's or what?"

"Ceci, what we did wasn't exactly sleeping," Bobbie said.

Ceci tried to sound business-like, efficient, secretarial, composed. Her mother sang in the background, "Play it how I may, I was made that way. I can't help it." "I really think that I should speak directly to Mr. Mason regarding his request. Thank you." She hung up. "What is wrong with you people?"

Bobbie said, "There's this new reality show. They give makeovers. I mean total makeovers. Give it some thought, you two. I have homework."

Ceci said, "You're an asshole."

"Yes, but I know that I am an asshole which makes me just this side of an asshole, more like a cheek. Cheeky." Bobbie winked at her and ducked down the hall.

Dee palmed her daughter's face. "You slept with him?"

Two days later when Ceci got back from Classic Video, Dee was at the Deco desk sorting through some old promo snapshots. She shoved aside the stack of albums on the table. "That Jason character didn't call back."

"Dee, that Jason character is never going to call back.

Never as in not ever. Never. Jason number two no doubt conveyed to Jason number three that our household is insane. Generally speaking, drama students prefer coaches who are not psychotic." She listened for the babble of the television. "Is Bobbie back from school?" She opened the cabinet and stared. Oatmeal. Nope. Baking soda. Corn meal. Did no one in this house ever buy food?

"He is not an attractive man," Dee said.

Duh. "That's the attraction. How old is this oatmeal?" That Quaker was looking a little faded, a little pinched.

Dee said, "I really have to find something professional to do. Maybe I'll schedule a dramatic reading. The library might be interested. I am an accomplished reader." She exhaled a wobbly smoke ring.

"Dee."

Bobbie banged in the front door. Ceci fidgeted with her bangs. Okay, his spider tattoo made her skin crawl, but still. . . . He was available.

"Look, you guys." The light winked off his glasses. "I think that I am going to have to move out. This isn't working."

Uh oh. "Are you giving notice?" Ceci asked.

Bobbie yanked the fridge open and stared. "Does anyone ever buy food?"

"You get room not board," Dee said. She stubbed out her cigarette. "I still think that that Jason character might call back."

"The horn of scanty," Bobbie said, considering a catsup bottle.

"Dee, he is *not* going to call back. Would you like a cup of tea?" Ceci asked. "We really depend on the rent you know."

"Tea and strumpets? No thanks." Bobbie slammed the fridge. "Truth is, I am thinking about a career in television."

Ceci tilted her head. One doesn't just leap into television. "Did you flunk out or something?"

Bobbie shoved his hands into his parachute pants. "Actually. . . ."

"I really do need a change," Dee said. "Maybe I should get back into theater. This," Dee gestured broadly, "is making me miserable."

"Yeah, yeah, marching to the beat of a different bummer," Bobbie said. "Dee, we've heard it all before."

"You did. You did flunk out, didn't you?" Ceci said. "I am really sorry." Stubbing his toes in his ballooning pants, he looked vulnerable suddenly, boyish, sheepish. "I am really sorry."

"I'm not," he said. "I mean, fuck, it's just community college. It's not like I flunked out of Harvard or something. I'm out of here," he said. And he was.

"I still think that that Jason guy might call. Or I should schedule a reading. I really should," Dee said. She glanced up at Ceci. "What's for dinner?"

Ceci tucked the cartons of Chinese food back into the fridge. Dee had eaten little of the General Tso's. Busy planning her reading. Jeez Louise. Ceci headed down the hall. Bobbie didn't answer the door the first time that she knocked. "I know that you are in there," she said. "I can hear the television."

Bobbie cracked the door. "And?"

"And I thought that you might like some dinner or that you could use some consolation."

"Consolation?" Colored lights whirled behind Bobbie like the Aurora Borealis. "Is that a euphemism for sex? You want to blow me maybe? Blow my dick?"

Ceci slumped. "Pathetic. Blow *you*? I don't even want to blow your nose. *Grow* up. Never mind." She turned away.

Dee's voice floated from the kitchen. "If I were you, I'd have nothing to do with that boy. Nothing at all. As far as I am concerned, he's free to leave any time."

Bobbie's glasses glinted. "Yeah, yeah. Freedom's just another word for nothing left to lose," he sang nasally. "By the way, Ceci, your mother never met Joplin. I mean, think about it. How old would she have been in 1970 when Joplin od'ed. Ten? What'd she do, meet Janis when she was ten? Give me a break." Bobbie shut the door.

Ceci stared at the grain in the oak. Lovely, Bobbie, lovely. "Reality TV?" she asked the door. "Try this on, Bobbie. Reality therapy. You are never going to make it in TV."

From the kitchen, Dee's shout wafted in on a blue raft of smoke. "He's a man way out there in the blue, riding on a smile and a shoeshine. Nobody dast blame this man. A salesman is got to dream, boy. It comes with the territory."

When Ceci entered the kitchen, Dee looked up at her brightly. "Arthur Miller," she said. "*Death of a Salesman*."

"Oh, shut up, Mom."

As Ceci expected, Dee's dramatic reading turned out not to be a great idea. Dee did in fact interest the local library in a reading with her list of credentials and performances without mentioning that most of them were twenty years old. And she did enlist Ceci in posting announcements and distributing fliers in local stores. And she did select a passage with sedulous seriousness. And she did expect various players from the Blue Angel to turn out to hear her. And she did fret over what to wear for days, finally settling on a blue velvet princess seamed hostess dress, pinched too tight in the waist, Ceci thought and too warm for the season, but she kept that to herself. And Dee did practice her soliloquy for several days before the parlor mirror, much to the irritation of Bobbie who had not yet moved out although he still intended to and who turned up the volume on the TV in a duel of pique.

Here's how it turned out:

Dee tanked up. Tarted up in the blue velvet dress, tipsy, slurry, and slightly listing at the lectern, she addressed four rows of chairs empty except for Ceci who had trouble concentrating, as she later told Bobbie, because the librarian, a trim blonde in eye-smarting Kelly green and hot pink, kept popping in and looking, well, appalled, and the other member of the audience, rumpled into a chair in the last row, a street person with Tourette's Syndrome kept yelling out enigmatic slogans. It was a little unnerving. And of course the members of the Blue Angel did not show up, likely because they had witnessed a few too many of Dee's sozzled soliloquies to find the unnatural disaster amusing any longer.

It sounded like this.

Dee: Whether tish nobler in the mind to shuffer

Rumpled Guy: (yelling) Copulating penguins.

Dee: The slings and arrows of outrageous fortune, Or to take arms against a she of troubles

Rumpled Guy: (louder) fornicating tuxedo birds on ice.

Dee: And by opposing, end them? Where was I? To die to sleep—
No more; and by opposing end them, and by a sheep

Rumpled Guy: Bleat, bleat.

Dee: To say we end the heartache and the thousand natural shocks.

Rumpled Guy: (muttering) fucking frozen birds and sheep. Bleat.

Dee: (faster) That flesh is heir to, tish a consummation, Devoutly to be wished. To sheep, perchance to dream; ay there's the rub

Rumpled Guy: Great rubbing penis-grabbing penguins.

And so on and so forth through despised love, a bare bodkin, to grunt and sweat all the way to the Nymph, in thy orisons.

Or so at least Ceci recounted it later to Bobbie in bed the night before he moved out of the bungalow, Bobbie who had shown up for Dee's reading, surprising Ceci even though he was late but not too late to help Ceci trundle Dee into the car and away from the librarian who, Bobbie agreed, looked appalled.

In the kitchen that evening Bobbie said to Dee, "You really should stop drinking."

Dee her chin, dismal in her propped hand, recited,

"Nothing is ever as simple as you think it's going to be. You take the simplest darn thing and, before you know it, it gets all loused up. I don't know how it happens or why it happens but it always happens."

She recited it perfectly, soberly, unslurrily. Clear elocution, impeccable emphases, with just the right tinge of wisdom, resignation, and despair, and added, "Richard in *The Seven Year Itch*." She struck a match and lit the filter end of her cigarette.

"Bravo," Bobbie said. He clapped listlessly. "But you're still a drunken has-been."

"And you," Dee said with a teetery gaze, "are a community college flunk-out." She sucked on her cigarette and then stared at it as if it were playing a practical joke on her.

"Another parable from the Book of Ruthless," Bobbie said and left for his room.

To which Ceci came shortly after bundling Dee to bed.

She knocked at his door. It cracked open. No TV.

"Well, this is a surprise," Bobbie said.

"You all packed?"

He swung the door wide. "Just about. The car's loaded except for what I'll need in the morning."

The room looked transient like the rumpled guy at the reading. "That was very nice of you to come to the reading. I mean even if it was a debacle."

Bobbie said, "It seemed like the right thing to do. I mean, I thought that you might need a hand."

"As it turns out," Ceci said.

"Do you want to come in?" Bobbie asked.

"I'd like to spend the night," Ceci said.

And she did.

In the morning Ceci wrapped herself in a chrysalis of Bobbie's top sheet. "I am going to miss you," she said.

"Word," Bobbie said, leaning over a box. He snapped off some strapping tape with his teeth.

"Why do you dislike us so much?" Ceci asked.

Bobbie turned around, propped his glasses on his forehead and blinked. "I don't dislike you. I just think that you are sad."

"I guess we are," Ceci said. She rose from the bed and embraced him quickly. "Years from now when you talk about this, and you will, be kind."

She did not tell Bobbie, "Laura in *Tea and Sympathy*." It was one of her favorites, a great scene, which she popped in from time to time at Classic Video when it was slow. She did not tell Bobbie that before he left, and she didn't tell him about the snapshot either, the one which she was looking at now of Janis Joplin, born in 1943 when "Mairzy Doats" was a hit song and the kids jitterbugged in Zoot suits, dead in 1970, a heroin overdose in the Landmark Hotel, the year of the Kent State murders, the year when the kids danced naked to "Aquarius." Janis is grinning, wearing sunglasses, an askew straw hat trying to tame her brambles of hair, and she is holding the hand of a small girl, maybe ten years old, who is staring, round-eyed and solemn, at the camera. The girl is wearing an Empire dress with a big bow, ankle socks, and Mary Janes. Her shoes are highly polished and the bow in her curls, pertly tied, looks somehow hopeful.

Cry Baby.

How To Stop Loving Someone

A Twelve Step Program

HERE'S HOW YOU DO IT. First, fall in love with someone. Anyone will do. A) the clerk in the convenience store, B) that man caressing a can of Save the Dolphins tuna, C) that long drink of water in the nubby Irish sweater eyeballing himself on the closed circuit TV. Select one. Preferably C). Send him yellow roses, Godiva chocolates, cashmere sweaters. Bake him pies. They prefer pumpkin. Get his phone number. Not necessarily in that order.

Second, talk on the phone. Be peppy. Make him laugh. At all costs, be interesting. More important, find him fascinating even when he talks about his skiing accident, his car accident, his socks, his war and love stories. Try to forget that the latter two equate; it will come in handy later. You will have a lot to forget.

Third, baste yourself and roast in a tanning booth. Do not get melanoma or wrinkles. Lose ten pounds and don't let them find you. Order lingerie from brown papered catalogues and wear it no matter how uncomfortable you find the thongs, and laces, and lace. Wear pearls without irony, heels without disclaimers or discomfort.

Buy dresses that you think he would buy for you if he bought you dresses. He won't. Let this be your mantra: if you want it (flowers, dresses, earrings, cute cards, pillow talk, reassurance, self esteem) do not wait. Not for a second. Run, don't walk. Jaywalk, jay-run, jay-hell-for-leather-at-breakneck speed hoof it to ensure it for yourself at the nearest florist/dress shop/jewelry store/ Holiday Inn seminar/ or self-help shelf in your local bookstore. The binding of love after forty is cracked and reads in Helvetica gilt font: DO IT YOURSELF. So do.

DO NOT talk about yourself, your former lovers, husbands, dilly-dalliances, or your offspring. DO NOT complain when you spend your birthday, Thanksgiving, Christmas, New Year's Eve, and Valentine's Day alone. (They hate that.) DO NOT analyze your relationship with him. They really hate that. Compliment him sincerely on his intelligence, hair cut, car and clothes, especially his socks (they give great thought to their socks) even if you don't mean it.

Go to his condo. Memorize his wardrobe, the tweeds, the double-breasted, gold-buttoned blazers that only he can wear without being flip or camp. Memorize the contents of his medicine cabinet. Run water while you click through his bottles of sinus spray, his prescriptions, the Valium, the Xanax. Rifle through his magazines, his CDs, his books. Always remember this: they secretly long to be rock stars. Or cowboys. They are desperate men. They play air guitar or air harmonica before the steamy bathroom mirror. They dream of room keys wrapped in red string bikinis tossed past the footlights. They dream of being lone little dogies eating maverick beans and fire-sizzled bacon. Their dreams are not their own. They secretly long to be rebels without a dependent clause, but only if, an essential if, they already have a girlfriend or a wife. They need their security systems.

Study the sock drawer. They take pride in the insignias. Other pod-women have gotten to them about the socks. No crews, only J. Crews, a discreet alligator, perhaps, or decorous tony Ralph Lauren argyles. Cull all the details. Become his expert. Memorize the photos of his mother, deceased father, his sister, his son, his girlfriend. Speak well of them all, especially the girlfriend. Compliment his taste in women. Never mind that she sells insurance, pays one hundred dollars a week for her hair and nails, drives a red car with a cellular phone. Study your rival. Cut your hair like hers. Forget the nails; you've most likely already bitten them to the quick. You will require a few nervous habits, however bad. Falling out of love is rigorous work. But that comes later.

Fourth, in bed strike a balance between demure and sluttish. Moan; they like that. Never, ever say, "Take me, take me, make me yours." They hate that. Tell him the truth, that he is beautiful, that his skin is soft and dark until the white band below his navel where you imagine enwrapping him like his swimsuit, that you almost cannot bear the auburn down on his abdomen, soft as it is, that his come tastes like strawberries, not the hothouse grocery store variety, the sun-warmed mid-July tiny ones which hide under parasol leaves of green. Put your index finger into his mouth like a key into a lock. It opens the door to that forbidden room where everything is tentative, where everything, perhaps joy, trembles and waits. His mouth is the threshold of possibility which demands great courage to cross. Cross. Cross over.

Kiss him. Exchange body fluids until you feel consumed, transubstantiated. Adore his bristly tree trunk of a leg between your thighs. Let your fingertips memorize the shape, the contour, the beautiful hardness of every muscle because you cannot help yourself, because you truly love this man, because you would sleep anywhere even on a bed of broken glass to hear this man's fitful snoring deprive you of sleep, because you cannot bear your own tenderness when you touch his sweet face, because you want to forgive him all his flaws, ease his past, take his pain into yourself and make it your own. Imprint his skin into your fingerprints until, defying nature, you are two snowflakes crystallized alike. And when he startles awake from his midnight ride on the white mare, console him, touch him until the white horse gallops off, touch him until, cocksure and cock hard, he rides you, saddles you with his pain although even he will not know that that is what he is doing.

When he calls you by his girlfriend's name, overlook it, overhear it. When he says your name, feel blessed by his voice. Let it haunt your dreams until you wake up in the morning and feel his fingernail, the crescent fingernail of his index finger, trace your backbone. Delude yourself that he loves you. Hook your pinky in the bliss between his lips, the bliss that is his mouth, the unuttered prayer that is always and only hope. Love him wholly, holy, sacramentally. Confess the sin of truth, that you have never known intimacy like this, so bottomless, so vast, as infinite as the chalice of your heart which you bear to him, offer to him. When he, in an anxiety of stage butterflies, drops papery like a Monarch's winter wings, lie. Tell him that it doesn't matter. Tell him that you are happy, satiated, full to the brim with him. Tell him until it becomes truth. It will be truth. It is truth. But learn how to lie. You will need to lie to protect him from himself, from his troubled past and inky dreams. Soothe him. Stroke his brow. Kiss his fingertips and say, "It's all right. Everything is going to be all right." Be his understudy. Become the biographer of his body. Always play Boswell to his Johnson.

Whatever else you do, do not cry. Do not cry even when you realize that anyone *won't* do. That only he will do, this one, him, him, himself, the one with the uptown argyles, the one with the ultraviolet ravaged face. Do not cry even when *them* redacts to *him*. Do not generalize, and never deign to become specific yourself. They hate that, and they really, really, really hate it when you cry. It makes them feel responsible.

Recall the mission of your education thus far. You have schooled yourself in him, tutored yourself in his dental floss, his scrapbook, his socks so that eventually you can stop loving him. Memorize his scent because you have no other choice; you will never be able to forget that he smells like anise and carnations, a day beyond their cut stem perfection. *Gillyflowers*. A scourge on memory. On love, on loving, a curse. But that comes later.

Fifth, ask nothing of him. You will get it anyway. Elate with an edgy joy when you spot a stranger who resembles him even in the most oblique way. Enroll in a dysfunctional relationship course, cram for the exam on Denial, carry crib notes about co-dependency, watch talk shows until your brain atrophies, gripe futilely to your therapist about men who fear intimacy. Read only

Chick LIT.. Glory in your victimization, but never ever allude to it. They really, really hate that. Remember: they are not accountable. They are not responsible for their actions. Sartre be damned, they know no bad faith. They lack free will; it is never their problem. Ever. Never. Not ever.

They blunder around among the heifers, stomping shards of Wedgewood into a pale blue dust beneath their hooves. It isn't their fault. It's how they're bred. Graze, stare dumbly, moo, make milk, nurse. If you still retain the capacity to frame even a fleeting thought, pray with all your cowness for artificial insemination to occur to your farmer. The herd goes on. Love falls by the byway. It's all for the best. You have several stomachs for grass, but you have no stomach for love. Don't worry. The diet will alter soon enough.

Sixth, ignore all of the above. Drink too much smoky Chardonnay. Call him after five when you know that his girlfriend is home. Recriminate him. Unleash the harpies who have become more crowded than the angels on a pin's head in the Pandora's box of your wounded loving. Mix your metaphors, mix it up. You are crazy with love, dizzy with longing, coiled with misplaced moonstruck lunatic unmet unmatched desire. It is not your fault; it is the nature of the beast. Moo, low. The blues are always down and dirty. Discover the gift that is your tongue. It terrifies him; it has known his teeth, his moistness, his fruited come. Say FUCK a lot. Talk like a truck driver, a stevedore, a Stella-deprived depraved man. They hate that; it isn't ladylike. Refer to yourself in the third person. Refer to yourself with self-hatred. Employ the venomous reductive C-word, the part that will not speak its name. Check a Georgia O'Keeffe coffee table book out of the library and feast your aggressive eyes on the female metaphors. When is an orchid not an orchid? When it's in a jar. Press against the glass bell jar that barely contains you. Kick in all the doors and roar like a whore, says Barnacle Bill the sailor. Avoid the temptation to sing Helen Reddy anthems, but do read Adrienne Rich. Dive into the wreck, ah, there's the ticket.

Feel sorry for yourself. Let him say, "Self-pity does not become you." You become it anyway. Suicide will slip its possibility like a blackmail letter into the envelope drop of your dark hour and dark heart. Go ahead, read it. It's only an aimless threat.

Accuse. Ecce homo. Unstring the pearls. Let toads and snakes and wet slimy primitives slither from your lips. Take Occam's razor to Bluebeard's twelve o'clock shadow. Let a frown be your penumbra. Scream, "I am not a convenience store. I am a woman." Let the ten pounds creep from the Pound and spring lapdog back into your lap. Weep. Rant. Gouge out your eyeliner. Slash your merry widows. Use your garter belts for sling shots and slay him with the arrows of outrageous misfortune. Disease your vocabulary. Call each other (here, he must participate) egregious names until the words coagulate, combine, amass weight, slide, slither, slink up the biological tree, develop legs, discover land, croak, tumesce into thunder lizards who will trample through the peat swamps of your tenderness, die violent, vicious deaths, sediment into the sheaved shale of hatred and provide you with fuel, more fuel, endless reserves of fuel to fire your madness which is the moon at which you will hopelessly howl.

That last step, step six, is absolutely, unqualifiedly essential. Without it, you cannot stumble. Without it, you cannot trip. Without it, you cannot bump down the stairs, acquire the bruises necessary to prove that you have loved and lost and can therefore attest that it is better to never love at all. Bruises fade. Can memory fade? Can memory fade enough that you can raise a parasol, shade yourself from pain? Maybe. Yes. Eventually. But that comes later.

Hang up on him, then call him back because you cannot help yourself, because you want his approval that your action, your tears, your bitter calls, your hurt letters preclude. Threaten him; you have no clout. Issue ultimata which will result in his dismissal of you. Let him complain, "You are forcing my decision." Let him gloat, "You will miss me." Tell him you already do, then hang up on him again. Brood for ten minutes, pace while you wait for him to call. When he doesn't, call him back. Many are called, but few are chosen. You will be one of the few. When he says that he hates to be pressed, when he says "I think of you as a sister," when he says "What happened to our friendship?" hang up again. Then hang up his picture in your bedroom. Keep another on your nightstand to punish yourself with longing, to prolong your self-torment. Repeat after yourself, "I don't have what I can't want." Fantasize only about him. Only he will suffice. In the wide desert of your white-sheeted bed, thirst until you hallucinate, see his figure wavering in the heat, a quaver, a quivering cipher. Oasis.

Check the mailbox for the letter which won't arrive. Then check it again and again until it becomes a nervous tic. Open and close the refrigerator. Stare at the unflashing Cyclopean eye of your answering machine. When your phone rings, bruise your shins in your scramble to answer it. When Joe the automated telemarketer pitches five-year light bulbs, spiral downward in a maelstrom of loathing at your expectancy, at your weakness. Check the mirror several times a day to be sure that you still exist. Rearrange your hair. You are never pretty enough. Eat the Havarti which you bought for him. The sound of your phone not ringing hums in your apartment, the silence so complete, so nearly complete that you startle when your neighbor's phone rings in the parallel universe beyond your white apartment walls. *She gets calls. She gets so many calls that she isn't even home to answer them.* You hear the dim formal electronic rhythms of her prerecorded message. You stare at the white wall as if it were an empty mirror, as if your loneliness were palindromic. If you could only ghost-walk through the wall, there, there on the other side, fortune would rise to meet you, come with both hands full.

Here is the still center. Here is the point to review, here before the long downward slide to the last step. The last one is a doozy.

"Say, where'd you meet him?"

"I met him at the convenience store. He turned around. He smiled at me. You get the picture?"

"Yes, we see."

Then what happened?

"That's when I fell for the litre of the pack."

So I called him. So he called me.

So then I go, "Let's get together?"

And he goes, "Yeah. Yeah. Yeah. We could have a swingin' time."

So I go and he goes, and it's love à go go. And he goes on and on, telling me about his tour of duty in Viet Nam, his failed marriage, his son who writes poetry and plays Kamikaze soccer.

He told me about the novel he was writing. He told me he loved Havarti. He told me about his socks. He did not tell me about the girlfriend. That came later.

How much later?

After I stopped resisting him, after we went out to dinner and sat outdoors holding hands at an Italian restaurant on a mountaintop, after we went swimming at midnight with fireflies, after I started loving him, after that.

And then? And then?

When he danced, he held me tight, and when he walked me home at night, all the stars were shining bright.

And then? And then?

And then he kissed me.

Did you love him right away?

No, I was afraid. Again? I thought, Love again? It is too painful. I can't, I can't free fall into love again,

But then? Then?

Yes. Then. I did.

And then and then?

And then lace fluttered in spring windows. Pansies sprang up in the windowboxes. I rose to him like a heliotrope to sun. I wove him viney into my hair. I kissed his eyelids. I kissed his perfect curled toes, every one. I loved him with every cell, with every pore, with every atom spiraling up the Diotima's ladder of my genetic material.

And then? And then?

Reader, he dumped me.

Seventh. Seven is a magic number. But if you have a tendency to bet on dark horses, it is not lucky. As you slip down the glass mountain, the three golden apples still intact and gleaming on its summit, you will notice that the downward slope is steeper, faster than the incline which was leisurely, which paused every so often to admire the widening view, the purling rivers, the skirling clouds, the tender pink light. The drop is sudden. The plummet quick. All love has a denouement, a declining sun; all stories resolve with a decrescendo, a diminuendo to silence. The downward slope. The spilled pail. *And Jill came tumbling after.*

Advice for the seventh stage: play only songs which remind you of him. Fall into a coma of disappointed love. Treasure your misery. Miss him at every turn. Grieve for him. Read Simone Weil's essay on love and underline key phrases in black ink like "Love is a sign of our wretchedness." or "Love tends to go further and further, but there is a limit. When the limit is passed love turns to hate." Pass the limit. Pass the time. Grieve for yourself. Forgive him, forgive everything except this: never forgive him for not loving you.

At this stage, you will call him again because you are in the habit of handing your life over to him. But you will do so less and less frequently. Sometimes you will hang up before you say hello. Sometimes you will listen to the electronic buzz of the phone after he hangs up. You will become a nuisance caller but only for a while. You will write him angry letters which you won't mail. You may drink too much Chardonnay for a while simply to make the days blur, pass with seeming speed, to drop a curtain between you and loss, between you and time.

At this point your heart will feel like a sparrow's terror beating its blind wings against the chimney flue. This is the time to observe the ritual of unloving someone. Remove his pictures from your wall and nightstand. Return his books, but don't enclose a note. Throw out his letters. Crate the few impersonal gifts he has given you: the used books, the secondhand CD's, the flying monkey, the watercolor of a birch tree, the pen and pencil set, the hand mirror. Remove the ring which is the only personal gift. Black onyx on a sterling band. Tuck it deep under the snarls of ironic pearls in your jewelry box. Take antacids. Ignore the physical symptom of thwarted longing, that ache, that hollow in your chest where your heart used to beat. Forget him even though you can't. Because you must. Because you are here, alone in this room, your head slightly tilted, gazing perhaps unseeingly out of a window at a sudden snowstorm as you remove an onyx ring from your finger. Because. Because. Because love always presumes an audience. Unfinished clause. You have only because. There is no other choice.

Eighth: erase his name in your address book. Stage revenge cycles in your daydreams: sending his love letters to his girlfriend, showing up at his tennis club with some handsome dope on your arm, adding his name to a computerized mailing list for neo-Nazis or the ever-emerging Christian right. (Surely by now they are emerged.) Hate him for denying you. Call him an asshole a hundred times a day. Be smug; he will never again be loved as much by anyone. Hope that he dies alone with pee stains on his designer pajamas.

If you must, break something, a tea cup, a glass, preferably break one which you never much cared for, maybe that one with Fred Flintstone's imbecilic grin on it. The glass makes a satisfying sound as it smacks on the kitchen floor and shivers around your bare feet. Tell yourself that you are better off without him. Tell yourself you don't need him. Tell yourself he's history, except . . . except. . . . Some days are darker than others.

Ninth, same as above only a milder attack, and the Havarti's all gone.

Tenth. Sometimes at odd moments he flashes, flickers like a goldfish through the glass bowl that contains your consciousness. A fragile moment. Think of him wryly. Think of him wistfully. Think, but just for the duration of the briefest kiss, how it might have been other, that alternate life, that life which you might have led together. Pies in the oven, dimity curtains in the window, him there in that navy blue wingchair reading one of his silly Technothrillers while you watch him with wifely fondness and your Golden Retriever lopes dopily across the yard and the blue flag Irises, the color of his eyes, spike up in the flower beds.

Eleventh: like ninth and tenth only a shade dimmer. The pain peels off like the scrims of mica sparkling on a granite boulder, paler and paler, thinner and thinner sheets of Isinglass. Un-loving is a process of exfoliation. Layer by layer, you get closer to the hard pebble that is your metamorphic heart, pressure-warped and heat-fused. You no longer call him just to hear his voice on the answering machine. You remember the box in the attic and are surprised as you unwrap the watercolor that it no longer pains you. Now that you no longer want to call him, you find that you could, that you could ask him how life is treating him, that you could bear to hear his girlfriend's name in his deep, measured voice. You try to recall her name. There it is: yes, Lissa. You actually could call him. But don't.

Hang the watercolor back up in the living room. Try to click through the wardrobe of your memory for his suits, the smell of his starched shirts only to find the closet empty, the gillyflower perfume wilted, and his socks lamenting their mates forever lost in the limbo of some fluorescent-buzzed Laundromat.

Discover that certain songs, Counting Crows' "Mr. Jones" perhaps, no longer make you cry, that instead you feel only the aura of that time, that discrete episode in your life as if it were lived by someone else, someone who once knew you very well, him perhaps. Shake your head as you marvel how once you thought your very life depended on a word, a word from him, a word that bore all the joy that is possible in this world. Yes. Yes. Yes, I do.

But No slammed the door on the mustiness of an empty closet.

There will be other surprises. When you reread Simone Weil, different phrases isolate themselves like, "To love purely is to consent to distance, it is to adore the distance between ourselves and that which we love." Love the middle distance; it is time. It is love itself. It is the peace of knowing that you have or once had the capacity to truly, truly love. And above all be prepared. Because just when you think that you are finally at long last over him; then, at that very moment the floor collapses as you realize that you love him still, that you always will, and that you cannot bear it. Fall into despair. Open the forbidden door where your monstrous grief crouches, chuckling.

How to Stop Loving Someone

Twelfth. So here we are which is to say that we are almost there. We are almost at the bottom, the nadir, the piedmont. We are stumbling through the foothills of affection, back through time, back to the beginning before Jack and Jill went up the hill, before you met him, before you loved him where love ceases and there is surcease from pain.

There is, you will realize now, only one way to stop loving someone. Admit that you are powerless. Admit that you are a puling, crawling, drooling weak-kneed sapsucker. How to stop loving someone? You can't. Snap out of it. Forget it. Give it up. You can't because you cannot sear your own memory, you cannot burn him like an insincere love letter, you cannot scorch him out of your soul. No matter where you turn, he is there, biding his time in the lobbies and corners of your life and dreams. The cure for love is lobotomy or this. There's always this:

If you have the heart for it, return to step one. Select someone, preferably B). Repeat the above.

Palimpsest

FOR THIRTY-TWO YEARS Caspar Weems, who was actually a novelist which he would have been happy to explain to anyone who asked but no one did, had written obituaries for *The Glad Rag*, the newspaper with the third largest circulation in Hobson's Choice which was a city dwindled to middling in size, once renowned for its production of tractor parts and for rendering duck fat, and for a small role which it played in the Revolutionary War when one of the duck fat forebears got a Redcoat General drunk on dandelion wine who then failed to show up for battle, but the tale may have been apocryphal.

Hobson's Choice, nestled in the corner of a riparian confluence and in its day a port for mill goods, woolens and paper, now found its geographic situation anachronistic, but it stubbornly hung on despite its once rackety brick mills gone rickety. A hospitable city, even a convivial one, it boasted many neighborhood bars along the waterfront which had persisted from the days when the mills were working and liked to see their working men happy—or drunk and belligerent and Friday night paycheck poor. Like Hobson's Choice itself, the bars, a string of them named for their owners—Paddy's, Bruno's, Red's, Ritchie's, Joe's, an infrequently frequented Abraham's—hung on with the tenacity of vetch.

Caspar was well-suited to Hobson's Choice, having served *The Glad Rag* with the same tare-like perseverance with which the bars had served the working men of Hobson's Choice. Caspar Weems was a solitary man, serious, sedulous about obituary writing which he considered an art, and he had studied the styles and tones of other funereal columns with artistic perspicacity, noting the range from the lugubrious to the lurid, from the lachrymose to the laudatory, from the solemn to the silly. Caspar favored the encomium. Whenever anyone inquired about his style, Caspar liked to remark that the difference between elegy and eulogy was a few vowels. But nobody inquired except one elderly coworker, Turnkey, given to hovering around the water cooler in the morning, downing dromedary volumes before his break as if lunch were a desert, and given, in the afternoons, to an affability unmarked by thirst, but one which gradually gave way to a drowse at his desk. To him, Caspar was able to deliver his imaginatively rehearsed line, but only to him, because Caspar alienated the rest of the staff, largely newcomers, young, fresh from graduate study in T-com, VI-com, Com, or J-school with their whisk broom haircuts and squinty glasses, their etiolated coffeehouse complexions, noire elegance and Dolce & Gabanna gabardine. Caspar did not converse; he blurted—brusque and hard-boiled as he imagined rough and tumble newsmen spoke. Sartorially, he aimed for rumpled as he imagined gritty newshounds dressed, tie askew, tails untucked, and he achieved it.

When the cappuccino and croissant guy came around in the morning, Caspar growled, "Give me a cup of Joe." At lunch he hit the Hobson's Choice Diner and ordered, from a waitress with an etched blue "Hannah" name tag, corned beef hash with poached eggs "and leave 'em runny." Always ketchup. Always on the side. Always with a legal pad on which he scribbled his novel, Palimpsest, with papery zeal as if he relished rustling or wanted someone to ask him what he was working on. But no one did.

After lunch, office, then home. In the office, a serviceable drudge of renovated cubicles on the second floor of an old warehouse, Caspar wrote out his obituaries either longhand or on a recalcitrant old Smith Corona with a sticky letter 'H'. Most of the obits, he wrote pre-mortem, doing the research himself on the doctors, philanthropists, duck fat family members, or tractor tycoons, and retired school teachers, and downplaying the sundry scandals since he ascribed to the panegyric school. Life might be yellow journalism, but the obituary page was white. Black and white with solemn Old English font.

The meaning of life, Caspar Weems knew, was death. And its text: the obit. Obit. Obitus. Obire: to go, to meet, to die. And the novel, Caspar believed, was an obituary form. (Hadn't he read somewhere that some eminent author had proclaimed it dead?) So Caspar transcribed all of his obituaries into his novel as well.

What Caspar's colleagues did not know (although Troy Fagan, City Desk, was soon to learn) was that he always wrote two versions of his obituaries, one a tribute, the other an exercise in some aspect of fiction writing, tone, plot, humor. He needed to keep his craft supple.

Today he was working on a pre-mortem for the publisher of *The Glad Rag*, a duck fat descendant, Claude VanMeer and was exploring the issue of tone.

He wrote:

Claude Chase VanMeer, age *, died peacefully on *, ** in his home in Marvin Gardens. Claude was born in 1957, the oldest son of Claude and Mildred VanMeer of the VanMeer Rendering Plant. Claude Senior founded *The Glad Rag* in 1946 after returning from his service in W.W.II.

Claude Junior became the publisher in 1973 after briefly attending VanMeer Community College where he was preparing for a career in law. *The Glad Rag* flourished under his management growing from a local newspaper which focused on community and social events to a competitive daily which covered local, state, and national news, incorporated an editorial page, and obituary column, and an amusements page.

A selectman from 1977 until his resignation in 1978, Claude Junior, like his father, was active in local and national charities, the Odd Fellows, the garden club, and the Loyal Order of the Otters. He was also a member of The Equestrians and a renowned horseman.

His hobbies, which included architecture, cartography, spoon collecting, and limericks, and the members of his family were his greatest joys.

He is survived by his lovely and loving wife, Jillian who resides at Marvin Gardens, and his son, Bruce who resides in San Francisco.

The funeral service will be held at * at * p.m. at the * Church.

Friends may call at * etc.

Then he wrote:

Thankfully Clod VanMeer died, having outlived everyone's patience and interest. Claude was born a fat duck, choking on the golden ladle in his beak. After being kicked out of every school he ever waddled through, including the Hobson's Choice Normal School and the one which his father bought just so he would be accepted *somewhere*, he inherited *The Glad Rag* from his father, the goose who laid the golden egg. Claude Redux promptly scrambled it adding a page of his addled editorials, a garden column by his Belladonna, Jillian and a page of insipid horoscopes and amusingly unfunny cartoons. More of a Minus Touch than a Midas one, he had the good sense, nonetheless, to discriminate at least once between Fool's Gold and the echt ore and to hire and retain yours truly, 24 carat and freshly graduated from Cornwall University, to write elegant restrained obituaries for the proto-dead.

He was the member of many prestigious and prodigious drinking clubs, among them: the Oddballs, and the Loyal Order of the Why-I-Otter-Punch-You-One-For-That. He was a renowned horse's ass, kicked out of the most exclusive drinking club in town, The Board of Selectmen, for mixing a vodka Martini.

Claude VanMeer was a dabbler in slumlordship, much loved by his tenants when he turned on the heat to commemorate Ground Hog's Day. His lord also enjoyed finding his way home from Bruno's where he played the spoons and improvised dirty lyrics to pop songs on karaoke night. His hobbies included: tomfoolery, skullduggery, pettifoggery, and rampant quackery.

He is survived by his loving wife, his indiscriminately loving, all-loving, loving wife, loving everyone from ambulance chasers to zookeepers, Jillian, the dull trull, the trull doll, the droll troll and his disinherited son.

Etc.

Caspar was in the habit of submitting his handwritten or poorly typed copy with its dropped aitches to Lois the secretary, long in the habit, and long in the tooth of the habit, thirty-two years. A technosaur, Caspar was not about to make a sudden adaptation to electronic evolution.

"Copy," he said as he crunched the pages at Lois who perched on her stool at an over-varnished counter, and he blew out the door and hastened home. Caspar's home, a three room apartment, crouched above Bruno's in a sooty late Victorian tenement with one bay window which beetled out over River Street like a hyperactive eyebrow. Sparse but lavish enough for Caspar's needs, a black and white television, an enameled kitchen table, a bed, an easy chair, and a dormitory style fridge furnished the flat. Caspar had never upgraded the television because he only watched old black and white films, mysteries, dramas, the occasional romance, and he had no need of a desk.

He had read that Faulkner (or maybe it was Thomas Wolfe?) used a refrigerator as his desk. Doing likewise, Caspar reasoned, might inspire him to write his magnum opus, but the refrigerator was a stretch. Caspar was short, 5' 4"; hence the compact icebox at which he dutifully wrote every night after watching reruns of *The Untouchables*.

This was Caspar's life. And this might have remained Caspar's life were it not for the event which was about to change it dramatically, even drastically, the event which occurred the following morning when Troy Fagan, City Desk, summoned Caspar to his office. Troy Fagan always referred to himself as "Troy Fagan, City Desk," preferring, so Caspar thought, to present himself as moveable goods, decor, rather than as a sentient being.

"Caspar, have a seat." Troy Fagan invited him into the office.

Caspar slumped into the nubby Hunter's Green club chair and considered Troy who, he thought, looked more like a missile every year and not at all like a desk, his dome polished, his torso straight and somber in a charcoal suit.

Troy leaned casually against his leather inlaid desktop and crossed his legs, exposing his tan argyles.

Nice detail for the novel, Caspar thought. Nice detail for an obit.

"How long you been with us now, Caspar?"

Caspar rubbed his head. Theatrical question. Troy knew the answer better than anyone. He stared at Troy.

How to Stop Loving Someone

"How long you been writing the obits now?" Troy extended his arm, yawned, and examined his fingernails.

Caspar shook his head. Troy knew the answer to that one too. Same question.

"It's time for a new assignment, don't you think?" Troy propped himself back on the desktop and blinked into the popping hiss of the tubular fluorescent bulb.

Caspar sat attentive. An old newsdog, he had a nose for news, and in the obit biz a newsman knew that the noose was news. He sniffed a bad wind, a new breeze, a whiff of the dying breed.

"Get out of the old routine?" Troy continued, staring at the ceiling. "Take a risk? Shake the lead out?" he asked the water-stained acoustic tile.

Caspar lunged forward in the chair. "Hey, Mac. Whad is this? The third degree? Twenty questions? Why the grilling, hotdog?" Caspar asked in reporter-ese which he delivered with a hint of Hollywood Brooklyn.

Troy snapped upright. He liked Caspar, he really did, but VanMeer had called that morning. Lois, the secretary, had typed the wrong copy and VanMeer was not amused. "Caspar, I am merely suggesting a new assignment, something worthy of your creative talents. You've dedicated yourself to that novel—"

"On page eighty-five thousand, two hundred and thirteen," Caspar said. "but I started it late in life; I'll be working backwards soon to get the early years. Novel writing, it's a bitch."

"Exactly," Troy said, "and it deserves recognition. You must not squander those years of dedication to the craft. You're wasting away in obits. Your heart is in the arts."

"Ya wanna read the novel? My stuff? Bet on my dark

horse? Hitch a ride on my hansom cab?" Caspar asked. "It's a work in progress."

"No, no, not before it's finished." Troy relaxed again against the desk. The fluorescent light ricocheted from his pate. "I am thinking of a special assignment, a top secret mission, literary in nature, a scoop that could scoop you up more than a few awards."

Caspar studied Troy's argyle socks; he had to get the details of the diamonds right. He was engaged in writing a naturalistic roman à clef of his own life as it was happening. He had a Proustian eye for detail but an aesthetic of present rather than past tense, more Swann's Day than Swann's Way. Sort of Joyce does Proust. Or *Every Day In The Life of Caspar Weems*. Slice of life, he was buying the loaf, one long baguette, Swann's *Book of Years*. But recorded daily. And minutely.

Double diamonds, they were, with black diagonals. "What kind of assignment you got in mind, head honcho?" he asked Troy's feet.

"Okay. Here it is. No one has ever succeeded. How about an interview with T.D. Pinchinger?"

Caspar jerked his head up. "T.D. Pinchinger? The novelist?"

Troy nodded.

Caspar rubbed his forehead, the argyles forgotten. "The recluse. No one has ever had an interview with T.D. Pinchinger."

"Precisely. That is why it would be such a coup."

Caspar cathedraled his fingers. "Hmm. And if I cannot get an interview? If the canary won't sing? If the blue bird of paradise won't crow? If the Bird Man's flown the coop de Grace? If. . . ."

"Gather material. Snoop. Write an exposé."

Caspar considered, hunching. "Yeah, Troy, no question, that'd be quite a feather in my cap, quite a sugar lump in the cup, and a shot in the shot glass. Expenses?"

Troy shook his head. "You'd be on your own."

"Salary?"

"Of course."

The fluorescent tube hummed and hissed.

"Who'd do the obits?"

"We'll get one of the kids."

"The cashmere kids?"

"They all are today, Caspar. That's what we got except for Turnkey."

"Turnkey?"

"The water cooler guy."

Caspar nodded. "Yeah, right." He sank himself deeper into the club chair to consider it. An interview with Pinchinger. Nobody but nobodaddy had ever had an interview with Pinchinger.

"So?" Troy asked.

Caspar clapped his hands on the arms of the chair. "You're on, Mack," Caspar said. "I'm game." And he shot up from the chair.

Troy straightened and shook his hand. "Good man," he said, ushering him to the door. Troy smiled sweetly as Caspar shut it behind him, not knowing that he'd just been had. The assignment was impossible.

T.D. Pinchinger was the greatest cult author in the country. No one had ever seen him, but a few had read some or all of the six novels: *Alpha*, *The Knave of Diamonds*, *Pinchinger on Pinchinger: A Memoir or (K)not*, *A Black I*,

Z, and *Liner Notes: A Novella*. Caspar set about his research of Pinchinger with the same fervor with which he attacked his novel, unsurprising since they quickly merged into one project. Caspar spent days in the library researching the Pinchinger family tree. (There was none.) And he recorded the minutiae of his failed research promptly in his novel.

Caspar spent days researching birth certificates. He found no T.D. Pinchinger. And this, too, he duly recorded in his novel.

Caspar ran voter registration checks, drivers' licenses, marriage certificates, telephone listings. Nothing. And undeterred he transcribed this as well into his burgeoning novel.

Pinchinger did not exist. Except. Except there were the novels. The awards for the novels. The reviews of the novels. Caspar had read them all, all six. Six books in search of an author.

He researched obit pages across the country. Still nothing, and this nothing he also recorded in his novel, lucubrating at his compact refrigerator cum desk. Not dead. Not alive.

And there had been that sensationalist memoir by that low-Lolita sketching in autistic prose some sordid consensual S and M with Pinchinger. But the real scandal there was the writing. Nonetheless Caspar tried to hunt her down, but dead-ended at the pen name, Venus Blue. Behind the lickerish shimmer of the name, no one. Had it been an opportunistic hoax? He had laced up his gloves only to find himself shadow boxing, sparring with gossamer partners. Initials and a pen name. A planet, a goddess. And a color or an emotional condition.

How to Stop Loving Someone

Caspar needed to think. And he decided to think at the Hobson's Choice Diner. As he banged into the diner, he noted the neon cursive above the door, "obson's Choice Diner." The 'H' had long ago given up its aspiration and gas. Caspar spun onto a stool at the counter.

How could he find someone who did not even exist? "Gimme a cup of Joe," he said to Hannah. Pinchinger was no more than a series of texts. He'd contacted his publisher and gotten no response. How can you solve a mystery without a clue. Or was Pinchinger a clue without a mystery? A nom de plume, a ghost-written fiction himself?

Something was bothering Caspar. The waitress. What was her name? Hannah, right, Hannah. A palindrome. Anna in the middle. It was the 'h' that was troubling Caspar, that 'h' that was missing in the diner sign, the 'h' sticking in the office typewriter. 'H', that little hammock of a letter. If you took 'h' out of Pinchinger, you got Pincinger. Pinc. Pin. (He felt like a butterfly pinned to Nabokov's lepidoptery board.) Pince. Pince-nez. Did that help?

No. Caspar slurped his coffee. 'H', a stuck 'h'. The Smith Corona, he needed that Smith Corona, and he needed it urgently. Caspar tossed a quarter on the counter. "There you go, doll."

"Wow. Thanks, big spender," Hannah said, mopping the counter.

"Did you know that the Egyptians trained baboons to wait tables?" Caspar asked.

Caspar set the old typewriter on the fridge. Lois hadn't put up much resistance when he'd gone to claim it. Even Turnkey used a monitor now. "W y did the ' ' stick?" he typed. "Pincinger."

He knew that there was some connection. But what?

In the morning, Caspar set off for the library with his novel stuffed under his arm. He had research to do. That heuristic letter 'h', the stuck key was key to unlocking Pinc(h)inger, the Hermetically sealed, Pinc(h)inger. 'H' was such an interesting letter, aspirated, sometimes silent, a letter not unlike the author himself who had recently penned liner notes for a garage band.

Caspar trundled down River Street. In Hobson's Choice it was impossible not to note the letter 'H'. Hobson's CHoice. And Hero sandwicHes. And Hot coffee. And the Hotel, and Hobby sHop, and the Hourly masses at the CatHolic CHurcH, and the Hydrants, and the Hazard sign on Horlick Street, and the kids playing HopscotcH, and the Hotdog stand on Hospice Hill. How had Caspar missed it all these years, these aitches of which he was suddenly aware as if 'enry 'iggins were his secret speech coach in an encoded universe where the letter 'h' Hypersignified.

The highjinks of the highhats on their high horses cHasing hedgehogs. He was drowning in meaning, a surfeit of meaning, meaning everywhere. What if everything signified? He'd noticed this week that even his food was straining to mean—mottoes on teatags, fortune cookies, bubblegum fortunes, cracker jacks with pithy adages, talking food, clamorous snacks but no decrypting device for a prize.

Caspar banged against the huge oak door of the Hobson's Choice library. "HusH," the librarian said as he entered.

Caspar headed straight for the reference section in

the hieratic stillness. The shelf marked under his hieroglyphic, 'H'. 'h' that ideogrammatic chair, or humped house with a chimney, home, hovel. Or a handheld scoop standing on end. Or 'H' a bridge between I-beams, a swing, a cartwheel of acrobatic appendages.

He dropped a tome of 'H' onto the library table with his novel. Thunk, thud. He thumbed through quickly: Hermeticism.

That was it. Pinchinger, the hermit, hermetically sealed, thrice greatest, Hermes Trismegistus. Here was his Rosetta Stone: Hermeticism.

T.D. Pinchinger, like the Egyptian god, Thoth, was author of hermetic writings, an inventor of a new way of writing, magically sealed off from public investigation to keep the vessel of his imagination airtight and Pinchinger the author distinct from Pinchinger the person.

In his novel Caspar penned a cartouche, circumscribing carefully inside his sovereign's name: Pinchinger. It was all starting to make sense. It was amazing what you could see when you were looking for it.

Caspar scribbled in his novel: Hermeticism. The cosmos has unity and is interdependent. The meaning of life can manifest in sudden divine revelation. Sympathy and antipathy unite the universe. And one key can unlock it.

Rosetta Stone: stuck key. The letter 'h'.

Note to myself: it is possible that Pinchinger does not exist at all and is only the written biography of himself, a pre-written obit.

Then he slammed the compendium of H shut and headed home.

As Caspar entered his apartment, the phone was ringing.

This would fail to startle in most lives, but in Caspar's life it was extraordinary. No one ever called him. The phone was for calling out not in.

Caspar barked in the mouthpiece, "Yeah?"

"Is this T.D. Pinchinger?"

Caspar paused. Kind of a peculiar coincidence. "No."

"Do I have the wrong number?"

"Who is this?" Caspar asked, playing it sly.

"Who is this?" the voice answered.

A voice, Caspar noted, rather raspy, dry, the sound of a hasp on a clasp. "Is this Pinchinger?" Caspar asked.

"Good God no. Turnkey here. Is this T.D. Pinchinger?"

Turnkey. Whatever did this mean? Caspar goggled the receiver, then slammed it down.

Turnkey was the opposite of stuck key. How was he key in all this? And why did he think that Caspar was Pinchinger? And why was Turnkey calling Pinchinger?

Caspar twisted all night in mazey dreams about Venus Blue and Turnkey. Her back was to Caspar in the dream, but he knew that it was she. She wore a string bikini of blue velvet. Turnkey stood next to the water cooler, drooling dropped aitches; parti-colored, they swirled to the floor. Pinchinger appeared and told him to fall in love, that love was the answer to our riddling hearts. *Remember Z*, Pinchinger said. *The importance of love in Z. You must remember; after all, you wrote it.* Pinchinger's head looked like an unfinished cartoon; he had no face.

By the time that he woke up, Caspar was convinced that he was Pinchinger, that he had written the novels, all of them, that they were part of the text of *Palimpsest*, his novel, which, in fact they were, since he had transcribed them as he read them into his ongoing roman à clef featuring himself as protagonist.

Caspar was exhausted, but he nonetheless crossed to the kitchen and emptied his wastebasket on the floor. He had to find some proof that he was indeed Pinchinger. He found envelopes addressed to occupant and Caspar Weems. Receipts for Caspar Weems. Coffee grounds, they could be anyone's. And crumpled sheets of papers with missing aitches. The H was the thing, Caspar was certain. It was possible that he was Caspar Weems thinking that he was Pinchinger who was thinking that he was Caspar Weems. How could he be certain who he was?

While Caspar was sorting through his trash, Turnkey was dialing numbers at random and asking the answerers if they were T.D. Pinchinger. Troy had decided that the assignment, so effective with Caspar, would work as well with the sot. Troy Fagan, City Desk, had stumbled upon the perfect means to coerce early retirement.

Caspar Weems was making his way along River Street to the 'obson's Choice Diner, stopping at every trash can to sort through the contents for clues. In a world where everything meant, he could afford to overlook nothing, no candy bar wrapper, no gas receipt. The world had gone text which he quickly noted in his novel. He was having difficulty writing fast enough—to take it all in, to record it all. He rolled along the street like wadded newspaper, more rumpled than was usual, his shirt untucked, his wool sweater a gnarl of dags.

At last he blew into the diner. Hannah sauntered over

with her coffee pot propped. "Yeah, yeah, a cup of Joe."

Caspar shook his head. "Skip the Java. Who am I, doll?" he asked.

"You're the quarter-tipper, babycakes," Hannah said.

"Am I T.D. Pinchinger, the reclusive cult novelist?"

"Honey, for all I care or know, you could be the Queen of England."

Caspar clapped his hands flat on the counter. This did not sit well. The Queen of England? He was having enough trouble being Caspar Weems being T.D.Pinchinger and possibly Caspar Weems again.

"T.D., eh? What does that stand for? Totally deranged?" Hannah nodded at the pot. "Want coffee?"

"Coffee?" Caspar was already wound up tighter than a typing ribbon. He stared at Hannah's name tag.

"Yeah, coffee."

His eyes felt glairied. He was having a vision, another Hermeticist divine transmission. The dream. Good Night Nurse, Hannah was Venus Blue. The blue tag. And it occurred to him for the first time that T.D. might be a woman like T.S. Elliot. Wait, no he was the guy. George was the woman, same last name, one L, one T. Okay, H.D. then, or whatever her name was.

Hannah bumped Caspar's shoulder. "Yo, Rainman, coffee?"

Caspar stared at Hannah. Really stared. Her eyes were name tag blue. Her lips were as red as red flannel hash. Caspar slumped. Aw. He felt as if he were running all soft at the edges, albuminous like he liked his eggs. Okay then, if he was Pinchinger and Pinchinger was a woman, he was a lesbian. That was all right; he was liberal in his views.

"Coffee?" Hannah asked again.

"I prefer not to," he said.

"Suit yourself."

Caspar smiled coquettishly and blinked and flushed. "We're supposed to get married," Caspar said. "You and me. Caspar and Hannah. T.D. and Venus. I know. I dreamed it. It is prophecy."

Hannah stopped, pivoted and smiled, coffee cocked before her like a pistol. "A double wedding, ain't that grand? Go rent the chapel."

And Caspar spun off the stool, dizzy with spinning and longing, and dashed out to do precisely that.

Up in Marvin Gardens, spelled just like in the board game with the historical misspelling intact, an 'i' rather than an 'e', Jillian and Claude were considering adding another house to the lot. The developer had thought that it would be cute to name the streets after the game.

"But Claude," Jillian said, "we already have one green house."

Claude sipped his Martini. "For God's sake, Jillian, try to get into the spirit of the thing. Take a risk. It's a game of chance. Green means go."

"Green means greed. Go ask Gatsby. Two Kelly green houses, Claude? That is pretty dicey."

"You mean Fitzgerald. Go ask Fitzgerald. Gatsby starred in it."

"That was Robert Redford."

Caspar Weems' dream had proven not to be prophetic after all. And Caspar was out the cost of a chapel and a chaplain and was pondering the meaning of a letter (not the 'i' and 'e' of Marvin Gardens) but the letter 'h' which now stood for Hannah and heart, and his was broken. Caspar was learning that love was not the answer to the riddling heart, but rather was the loneliest place in the universe, lonelier than a treeless lunar plain, a vastness that knew no edges, that while it could (like the letter 'h') confer meaning, it could also deprive life of meaning (like a stuck key). And Caspar was stuck in the key of blue and typing Hannah's name (anna, anna) into his novel and pre-writing his obituary, the obituary of Caspar Weems who had for thirty-two years served *The Glad Rag* not the obituary of T.D. Pinchinger who Caspar could not be since Hannah was not the Venus Blue of his dream.

Caspar tapped the keys. He wished that love were more like his novel, encompassing, inclusive. But love, unlike, Caspar's art was selective. It selected one, and in that single and singular selection rejected an infinite number of other possible selections. Caspar was one of the infinite rejections. Hannah had turned him down flat. And Caspar had downed enough Xanax that he could actually *be* Club Med.

And then the phone rang.

"Yeah?"

"Is this T.D. Pinchinger?"

Caspar dropped the receiver. What a coincidence. Once a fluke. But twice? What were the chances? And then Caspar Weems had another aperçu.

He depressed the button and dialed information for Hobson's Choice. "Yes, I'd like the listing for T.D. Pinchinger," he said.

"We are sorry, sir. That number is unlisted."

"Thank you. Thank you so much."

Then he could be Pinchinger. Caspar capered on the kitchen floor around his fridge. Forgetting his novel, he rushed to the door. There was still a chance to woo his Venus Blue. And he could interview himself and publish it in *The Glad Rag.* Everything was falling into place. He paused. Perhaps he should double check, maybe look up Caspar Weems' number in the phone book. No, because he could still be Caspar Weems and Pinchinger, right, if Pinchinger's number was unlisted. The world, life and love, hinged on the meaning of the letter 'h'. Hannah was the meaning. Hannah was the answer. "H," Caspar yelled, "happy."

The god Thoth, inventor of writing, laughed. "Hah," he said. Or "Huh?"

Acknowledgments

"The Folly of Being Comforted," "What It Is," and "How to Stop Loving Someone," all appeared in *TriQuarterly*. "What It Is" also appeared in *Pushcart Prize XXVIII*. "Men in Brown" appeared in *GlimmerTrain*. "The Wig" appeared in *Manoa*; "The Writing on the Wall" in *The Dickinson Review*; "Tidewalk" in *The Ohio Review*; "Half-baby" in *The Southern Review*; "The Fox" in *North Dakota Quarterly*; "If It's Bad It Happens to Me" in *Hunger Mountain*; "The Landmark Hotel" in *The Antioch Review*; "Palimpsest" in *The Gettysburg Review*; and "Aground" appeared in *The North American Review*. It later won *The Ohio Writer* award where it also appeared.